Praise for

K. M. Mahoney

...a fast-paced, action-packed adventure in hide and seek exploits, spaceship battles, galaxy jumps and hilarious commentary...steamy intimate scenes as well as emotional insecurities. ~ *Literary Nymphs Reviews*

*Total-E-Bound Publishing books by K. M. Mahoney:*

In Teddy's Arms
Odd Man In

# ODD MAN IN

K.M. MAHONEY

Odd Man In
ISBN # 978-0-85715-762-1

Interior text design by Claire Siemaszkiewicz
Total-E-Bound Publishing



Published in 2011 by Total-E-Bound Publishing, Think Tank, Ruston Way, Lincoln, LN6 7FL, United Kingdom.



Total-E-Bound Publishing is an imprint of Total-E-Ntwined Limited.



Manufactured in the USA.

# ODD MAN IN

# Dedication

To Mika and Roxy, the inspiration that helped bring Terran to life.

# Chapter One

It wasn't the first time he'd been snagged. And it wouldn't be the last time, either. Daior Mathews had been told on many occasions he had a real problem with authority. He always replied that it wasn't a problem but a really intense distaste. Authority and organisations. And politicians. And dentists. He wasn't too fond of dentists. Hell, he didn't like anybody, really.

So when the guards opened the door and tossed him a companion, the kid flying through the air like a freaking trapeze artist—with the greatest of ease and a really hard landing—Dai should have minded his own business. Could have. Should have. The story of his life.

But Daior just never learnt. When that kid hit the ground at his feet, looked up at him with those pale blue eyes... *Hell.* Daior had a feeling his life had just become a great deal more complicated.

He sighed, leaned over, grabbed the kid by the shoulder and hoisted him upright.

"Kid," he said. "Didn't anyone ever tell you that you need wings to fly?"

The kid dusted himself off. "People keep saying that."

"And you keep trying to prove them wrong?"

"Something like that."

Daior snorted. The kid had quite a mouth on him. Daior liked it.

The kid grinned at the sound. "I'm Terran," he said. He tilted his head back, studying the grey stone arching over their heads. "So, where are we, and how do we get out?"

"We're in a private complex on an unnamed planet in the Delta Sector."

In Daior's opinion, 'planet' was being generous. The blasted rock was way too small to manage enough gravity for a stationary orbit or a semi-comfortable living environment. Heck, he'd seen asteroids larger. It must have one hell of a density to make up for it. Daior had pretty much covered the whole thing during his last escape attempt. It had only taken him about twelve hours, with the exception of the blasted mountain. No way was he climbing a mountain. That part he'd left unexplored. Nature wasn't really his thing.

Terran kicked at the wall, crossing his arms and scowling. He was probably attempting to look ferocious, but his features were far too fine and, well, cute for that. "This wasn't exactly how I planned to spend my weekend."

Daior watched bits of rock skitter across the rough floor and his mouth quirked. "Not exactly my idea of a good time, either."

"You never answered my other question," Terran pointed out.

"What question was that?" Daior could feign ignorance with the best of them.

"How do we get out?"

"We don't."

Terran started chewing on his lip, foot jiggling nervously. "What do you mean, we don't?"

"This planet's about as big around as a nutshell. No place to hide. And no available ships to get us off, either. We're effectively stuck."

"Well, what do they want?"

"With me? Something they aren't gonna get. You? Damned if I know."

Terran wrapped long fingers around his slender hips and glared, his blue eyes like icy fire. "What *do* you know?"

"That you're damned cute when you're mad."

Terran's mouth dropped open, and Daior half expected him to stomp his foot.

It was the truth, though. The light wasn't very good—KoraGel lamps might be convenient and cheap, but they were crappy for lighting anything larger than a one-person tent. The six bolted into the stone walls of their cave barely kept the dark at bay. Even so, he could tell the kid was something else. Small and lithe but nicely muscled. Built for speed and agility, not strength and persistence, like Dai was. Hair of some indeterminate shade—light but not blond—stuck up in neat spikes. A pert nose, rounded cheeks with cute little dimples—hell, everything about the man was little. Except for those eyes. They were big, expressive and the prettiest shade of blue Daior had ever seen. Bright with life and enthusiasm and glittering like the heart of a nebula.

Those eyes suddenly lost their sparkle. It hit his gut hard to see it go.

Terran sighed and plopped down on a large rock against the wall, resting his chin in his hand. He didn't say anything, just stared at the shadows lurking around his bare feet.

"Where are your shoes, kid?" Daior asked.

"They took them."

"Why?" he asked with honest confusion, casting a look at his own boot-clad feet.

"I don't know. I don't know who they are or what they want with me or anything. I was just out having a few drinks, wandering around Quentain, and suddenly I get kidnapped. I guess I should just be glad they only took my shoes. That ugly guy wanted to take my clothes, too."

"They're all ugly," Daior replied absently. But... *Well, damn.* He probably wouldn't have minded a naked Terran all that much. Or at all. *Wait...Quentain?* If Daior's calculations were correct, they were currently on the fringes of colonised space. Quentain wasn't even in this galaxy, let alone the same solar system. They must have wanted Terran badly to drag him that far. Either that, or they really, really didn't want to be found. Maybe both.

Daior pushed aside the questions for the moment. At the same time, he tried to bury the instant surge of lust that had his cock hardening in his battered cargo pants. Just because he'd been stuck in here for far too long, and in deep space for months before that, didn't mean his control was completely shot. He could restrain himself from falling on the first cute twink he came across.

*Maybe. Probably.* And hell, nothing even guaranteed the kid was gay, anyway. Although his gut said yes. Loudly. And Daior's gut was usually right.

Daior slid down the wall until his bum hit the floor, and he stretched out his legs, crossing his ankles and settling in. He didn't bother trying to get comfortable. It would be a wasted effort.

The silence started to lengthen between them, awkward and heavy. Daior cleared his throat.

"Where are your folks, kid?"

"I'm not a kid," came the mumbled reply.

"Sure. You're what, all of sixteen?"

"I'm twenty-two," Terran replied indignantly.

*Oh, happy day.*

"You never told me your name," Terran pointed out.

"Daior Mathews," he replied. He picked up a bit of rock, rolling it absently between his fingers. "Dai or Mathews will do."

"Nice to meet you," Terran murmured automatically, as if it were ingrained in him to be polite.

With Terran's fine bone structure, it probably was. Terran had the appearance of upper class about him. Daior knew that look. He'd been employed by more than a few of them in his time. Not around here, though. This part of the universe was mostly mining and farming communities, colonised settlements. Lots of trading ports, slums and the occasional pirate to make things interesting. The powerful, so-called 'civilised' planets were farther out, a couple of galaxies over and to the left, if Daior's direction sense wasn't completely screwed up.

"So, what?" Terran demanded. "They're just going to keep us locked up here forever?"

"Nah. They want something."

"What?"

That one made Daior pause. How much to tell the kid? For all he knew, Terran had been dumped in to go digging for information. Didn't explain the lack of shoes, but Daior decided to play it safe and stick with the basics.

"I'm a Tek," he replied. "Let's just say they've taken a lot of X-rays and hooked me up to a couple of mainframes."

"A Tek?" Terran's brow furrowed in confusion. "But—"

Daior's arched brow dared Terran to ask more questions. Terran was not, apparently, an idiot. Those lush lips closed just as quickly as they had opened. Not that Daior didn't know what Terran had been going to ask, anyway. Why him? Teks were a dime a dozen. Everybody and their pet had some form of technological enhancement these days, even if it was just a basic intelligence augmentation. But further details fell under the 'better safe than sorry' category.

"Soooooo." Terran drew out the word until it had about ten syllables. "What do you do for fun around here?"

"It's dark, damp and I've been stuck by myself. What do you think?"

"I Spy?"

"Smart mouth."

Terran snickered. "Yep, that's me."

Daior sighed and tilted his head back, staring sightlessly at the ceiling. "They have a routine," he said. "Never varies. Food twice a day. Facilities are in the back." He jerked his finger to a corner of the room. A small alcove contained a toilet and sink. Standard ship-issue, basic and cheap.

Terran's eyes narrowed speculatively at the equipment.

"No removable parts," Daior told him.

"They're just no fun at all, are they?"

"Not in the least."

Terran sighed, a big puff of air that made muscles shift tantalisingly under his thin T-shirt. "My brother will come," he stated. "Eventually."

"If he can find us," Daior pointed out. "We're pretty far off any main trades routes, and there's minimal technology, making us next to impossible to scan for."

"Oh, he'll find us," Terran stated with complete confidence. "Richard has a lot of really nifty, expensive toys. I'm just not sure I want to wait for however long it's going to take."

"We might have to." Daior hated to burst Terran's little optimistic bubble, but better he knew the facts now. "I could probably get us out of the facility, but after that there's nowhere to hide. And there's damn sure no way off the planet. No port, and the only interstellar ship belongs to whatever group is currently offering us their oh-so-gracious hospitality. It never sticks around long, just to drop off supplies and the occasional person before taking off again."

"Can't we just, I don't know, hide out in the jungle or something until Richard shows up?"

"This planet's pretty wild." Dai wasn't big on camping. And damn if he wasn't starting to feel like the bad news messenger. Couldn't Terran ask him a question he could answer positively? "The town is tiny, the surrounding area mostly forested wilderness and that blasted, impenetrable mountain range. Lots of big carnivorous creatures and not a lot of food."

"Sheesh," Terran muttered. "And here I thought Richard was Mr Gloom and Doom."

Daior shrugged. He didn't go in for sugar-coating or soothing. He had given Terran the truth. It wasn't Daior's fault the truth wasn't exactly rosy.

Daior had made a pretty thorough study of the place on his first escape, about twenty-four hours after they first scuttled his ship, stuck him with a tranquiliser and hauled him here. Daior had evaded the guards for nearly twelve hours while he conducted his survey. Then he'd let the bastards haul his arse back, figuring he might as well wait and plot in semi-comfort. Or at least with a roof over his head and food for which he didn't have to scrounge.

The compound itself was small and clearly privately funded. It sprawled along the base of the mountain, buried in stone in several places. Protection, he figured. Their cell was part of that, one of a small series of rooms off a back hallway that burrowed under the protruding edge of the comparatively tiny mountain. The entire place was quiet, secluded. So far, Daior had seen only a handful of staff, mainly medical personnel, and maybe a dozen guards, none uniformed. Or at least, not wearing any government or Fed uniform. And it wasn't like the Federation really cared too much about one lone Tek. They had their hands full quelling rebellions and averting world disasters.

If there was one trait Daior possessed in overabundance, it was curiosity. The last few days, there'd been a feeling of anticipation in the air. The bastards were waiting for something. Now that Terran was here, Daior suspected things would start happening. Their captors had what they needed, although damned if Daior knew what they intended to do with it.

But looking over at that attractive face, those pretty eyes, Daior decided he certainly intended to find out.

Terran studied his cellmate from under hooded lashes. He licked his lips and swallowed a little purr of approval that tried to work its way free. That was one fine hunk of man sitting in the shadows. Not huge or incredibly tall but nicely muscled. Dai's shirt stretched tightly enough to outline a nice set of pecs, arms bugling tantalisingly. An intricate tattoo traced its way around his wrist and wrapped around his lower arm, the lines curving in patterns that Terran badly wanted to trace with his fingers. Dai's face wasn't anything spectacular, sharp features with dark, brooding eyes. Firm lips that, while entirely kissable, could definitely stand to smile a bit more. Not that Terran could see them all that well, what with the fuzzy growth of wild beard that covered the lower half of Dai's face. But that body… That, and the wild thatch of curly, dark hair that Terran just wanted to sink his fingers into. The strands would twist so nicely around his grip.

A loud thud in the hallway made Terran jump, jolted unpleasantly back to reality. And while reality did include the lovely eye-candy on the other side of their small cell, it also contained…well, a cell.

Terran absently flexed his hands. His fingers itched and his body ached as he replayed the previous day's events in his mind. The big jerks coming out of the alley, the sting in his neck as they'd tranqued him. He didn't remember much of the transport from Quentain to wherever the heck he was now. For all he knew, it had been a lot longer than a day. And however long it had taken, it hadn't been an easy trip, he knew that much. Terran ached from head to toe and just knew there were some beautiful bruises under his clothes. He aimed a string of malicious thoughts at the jerks who'd grabbed him.

Why him? For once, Terran had been minding his own business. He'd just finished up a lovely night of debauchery and was heading back to his brother's ship…

His brother. Oh, Richard was going to be royally pissed off. At Terran, of course, because Richard seemed to believe every disaster, major or minor, could be blamed on Terran.

Terran had been trapped aboard a deep-space Voyager with his brother for nearly five years now. Five long, frustrating years, travelling from planet to planet while Richard did…whatever the heck it was he did. It usually involved long, boring diplomatic dinners that Terran was far too often forced to attend. Parties were not, unfortunately, always fun. Was it any wonder he kept sneaking off for some good times? Wasn't as if he could get any under his brother's watchful eye.

Ever since Terran had hit puberty and some of his peculiarities had become evident, he'd been living with his brother. Richard was nearly ten years older than Terran and took the word 'responsibility' far too seriously. He seemed to feel it was his duty in life to curtail Terran's activities. Richard had an irritating aversion to anything Terran considered fun.

The fact that a lot of Terran's fun activities ended up with him arse-deep in trouble was, of course, beside the point. Not that Richard agreed, of course. He threatened on a nearly daily basis to ship Terran back to Altaireon. And that just wouldn't do. The only thing less fun than diplomatic dinners was being stuck at home attending political functions and royal balls. Besides, Terran's mom would start trying to marry him off again. The very thought made Terran shudder.

"You're growling," Terran's big cellmate pointed out in even tones. He could have been asking Terran to pass the salt.

"Sorry," Terran said with a small shrug.

"What are you thinking about so hard over there?"

"Our situation."

"Don't," Daior advised. "You'll just give yourself a headache. Not much we can do right now. Just sit tight and wait for an opportunity."

"An opportunity? We might not have that much time. You said you've been here for a week and you haven't found one yet." Terran tried to point out the fact without sounding too accusing. No sense pissing off Daior if he could help it.

Daior shrugged, not seeming to take any offence. "Haven't really been looking all that hard."

"Well, why ever not?"

"Everyone needs a hobby?"

The sentence came out as a question rather than a statement. Terran wrinkled his nose. "That makes absolutely no sense at all."

One corner of Daior's mouth tipped up, creating interesting brackets along the sides of his firm lips. "Didn't say it did."

"You're a strange, strange man."

"So they say."

Daior fell silent. He kept watching Terran, though, with an intense regard that sent a small shudder rippling up Terran's spine. Terran licked his lips, body reacting to the heat in Daior's eyes. Opportunity? To heck with that. Terran could think of much better things to do with *his* time than sit around here. Of course, most of them involved a large bed and the man sprawled with arrogant machismo across from him.

Terran didn't have the patience to wait for their captors to slip up, give them an opening to escape. Terran usually created his own opportunities, not wait for them to be handed to him.

The logical part of his brain chose that moment to pipe up and remind Terran of what generally occurred *after* he'd created his own opportunities. That same part of his brain said maybe he should listen to the sexy man.

Of course, as soon as the thought occurred to him, Terran discarded it. He hadn't listened to anyone in years and wasn't about to start now.

Still watching Daior from the corner of his eye, Terran began to plot. He did like to plot, and at the moment, he had two goals to work towards—escaping their current predicament and finding out just how Dai tasted.

# Chapter Two

"King me," Terran crowed triumphantly.

"I thought we were playing chess."

"Hey, you play your game and I'll play mine."

Daior snorted. "I'm pretty sure it works better if we both play the same game."

Terran surveyed the collection of rocks spread out between them. "Which ones were the knights?"

"Heck if I know."

Terran surveyed the makeshift game board with distaste. He *itched*. His legs were jittery, body wanting to get up and pace. Or, better yet, run. According to Richard, Terran was overly fond of small, enclosed spaces. Terran wouldn't disagree. He just didn't like being trapped. At all.

For some reason, Terran's big cellmate didn't seem to care that they were locked up, waiting for whatever was going to happen to, well, happen. No, the big jerk just sat there. And played *chess*.

Terran had tried to pull Daior into plotting sessions but with an infuriating lack of success. Okay, so some of Terran's ideas weren't the most practical solutions. But if Dai were going to shoot them all down, the least he could do would be to propose some alternate ideas. No. Instead, the man proposed *chess*.

Terran was all for distraction. But if he were going to be distracted, there were far better methods than board games. Unfortunately, Daior didn't seem interested in those methods any more than he was in escape.

Glaring across the few feet separating them, Terran continued his inner debate. Was Daior dense, playing hard to get or just plain not interested? The dense argument, well, Dai would have to be really, really dense. Because Terran was generally not a subtle person when it came to sex. Over the last twenty-four hours, his innuendos and flirting had taken on a blunt, hammer to the head approach. And still the man kept talking about board games. And Terran's past, which Terran had very little inclination to discuss. Daior wanted to get to know him? Fantastic. No better way than a hot, sweaty make-out session.

"You don't really want to play chess, do you?" Terran asked.

Silence. Daior had that blank look on his face again, the one that usually meant he was off somewhere else in his head. Not paying attention. Terran resisted the urge kick him.

"Dai?" By the third time Terran called the man's name, he wasn't able to keep the annoyed edge out of his voice.

Daior jerked. "Yeah, kid?" he asked gruffly.

Terran hefted the rock he'd been fingering—he thought it was supposed to be a pawn, rather appropriate, that—and chucked it at the wall, then watched as it dissolved into a puff of dust on contact. "I'm bored," he declared.

"That makes two of us."

Terran tipped his head back, staring at the ceiling. And was the stupid arch of rock closer than it had been before? No, it was probably just him. The room wasn't really closing in. He just needed to remember that.

"I don't like being cooped up," Terran complained. "Makes me edgy."

"Patience," Daior counselled.

"I don't do patience well. I want *out*!" Terran swallowed the growl trying to work its way up from his toes.

"And where are you going to go?" Daior pointed out. "There's no transportation off this damn rock. You'll be back here within the hour and probably in far less comfortable circumstances."

Because a cave-like cell was so very comfortable. Terran forced himself off that track. He wasn't going to get snarky with Daior, he wasn't. But it had been…how many days now? Let's see, they'd snatched him approximately forty-eight standard hours ago, but had he remembered to take his medication that day? Shit, he hadn't. No wonder he was so edgy. A few more hours and Daior was going to get to see really snarky, and there was going to be little Terran could do about it. Most of his genetic issues he could deal with, control. But the mood swings? They were an utter bitch.

"We need to at least try *something,*" Terran insisted. Before the situation spiralled completely out of control. His mind hopped from one plan to another, mixing and discarding, thoughts moving faster and faster as his energy level spiked. "Oh! I know. I'll pretend to be sick. Then you can hit the guard over the head and—"

"Kid, I don't think that trick has ever worked, in all of recorded history."

"You never know." Terran bounced to his feet, flushed with the thought of pending success. "I'm gonna try it."

Terran didn't see Daior stand up, didn't even see the bigger man move, but suddenly his shoulder was snagged, jerking him to a halt with such force his feet nearly flew out from under him.

"No way," Daior snarled. "We are going to sit here like good little prisoners."

Terran's excitement drained away in the face of Dai's disapproval. It was all he could do to keep from drooping.

"I've never been good in my life," he muttered to the floor.

Terran knew his own flaws. He was determined, stubborn and prone to being hyperactive. He talked too much and tended to bounce from one thing to another without stopping for breath. He often came across as forceful and, at times, obnoxious. He didn't mean to. It wasn't his fault that most people couldn't keep up with him. Wasn't his fault that he was different, that his mind worked oddly.

Daior used his grip on Terran's shoulder to shove him back to the floor. Terran would have got pissy, except Daior was gentle about it and lowered his own bulkier frame down beside Terran, close enough this time so Terran could feel the heat from his body. It felt wonderful, and Daior smelt good and Terran really, really wanted to be distracted. If Daior wasn't going to let him attempt an escape, then Terran needed to occupy himself. Because otherwise? His overactive imagination was going to start in on depressing thoughts and worst-case scenarios, and then he was going to start panicking. And him panicky? That was never a good thing.

Terran slid a little bit closer, licking his lips. His seduction attempts might not have worked the first couple of times, but Terran was never one to give up without a fight. He wanted Daior, a lot. And at the moment, he really couldn't think of a better way to distract himself, either.

He opened his mouth to speak when something caught his attention. Terran pretended to be pouting, glancing up and sideways from the corner of his eye. There, on the wall, a red light had begun blinking. *Well, shit.* He narrowed his gaze on the surrounding wall, pupils dilating, studying carefully without being obvious.

*Oh. Oh, those bastards. A camera. Well, hell.* That sort of deflated a lot of his plans, now, didn't it? The thought of the guards watching was better than a dunk in an icy lake on his previously stirring erection. And how the heck was he supposed to debate escape plans with Daior when their captors could be listening to every word?

Dai seemed completely oblivious to their audience. Terran didn't really want to point and say, 'hey, they're watching us, how about that?' Terran wasn't sure, but it seemed like it could work to his advantage somehow, if he knew they were watching but they didn't know that he knew…and that sentence was a mess and made his head hurt.

*Oh.* A thought popped into his head and Terran had to press his lips together to contain a wicked smile. Fun and games, drive both the guards and Daior nuts at the same time, what wasn't to love?

The expression on Dai's face when Terran launched himself against the other man's chest was priceless. Dai grabbed him, steadying them both even while he tried to push Terran away. Terran, though, wasn't having any of that. He wrapped his fingers into the shaggy hair at the base of Daior's neck and took the kiss he'd wanted for days now.

Knowing they were being watched took away a lot of the pleasure of the embrace, but Terran still found himself purring, pressing close. Daior resisted briefly before opening his mouth, letting Terran explore a bit. Terran wriggled, and the next thing he knew, Dai was trying to consume him. Dai flicked his talented tongue across Terran's lips, teasing, and explored his teeth. A beard brushed against Terran's skin with a nearly ticklish softness. Terran lost himself in the kiss for a moment, briefly forgetting the whole point of getting so up close and personal with his cellmate.

The light on the camera started to flash, though, and it jerked him back to his ultimate goal. Terran pulled his lips away, albeit reluctantly, and nuzzled into Daior's neck. He slid up, still pretending to be lost in a sexual haze, until he could whisper directly into Dai's ear, so close that not even the most advanced camera microphone would be able to pick it up.

"They're watching us."

"Huh?"

Terran really wished they were somewhere else, anywhere else, so he could truly enjoy the lust-filled daze on Dai's face.

"Camera, back wall, half-way up, just above the ledge."

Terran tried to keep his voice even as he recited the facts and must have succeeded, because Dai's face sobered. However, Terran really could have done without the annoyance tinged with disgust that he got. Shit, he hadn't thought Dai would actually believe Terran was only playing him.

"Yeah," Dai murmured. He still held Terran close but had stopped moving his big hands. "It's not always on, though. Plus, it's a cheap thing. Limited line of sight. Keep to the walls and it has trouble picking up a clear video."

"What about audio?"

"Doesn't have any. I checked."

Terran eyed the wall dubiously. "How the heck did you manage that?"

"I haven't always been a transport pilot," Daior replied vaguely.

"What were you, a mountain goat?"

And Terran was starting to feel cross and irritable again. *Damn it all. That was...way too fast.* Far faster than it should have been, the upswing and subsequent drop.

He realised Daior was still talking and tuned in to hear, "...Advanced Tek mercenary."

"Sorry, run that by me again?"

"I said, I was a specialised mercenary, complete with advanced computer systems. Turned 'em off about ten years ago, but that doesn't negate decades of training and experience."

"Oh."

*Oh, shit.* Terran's mind had been leaping around again. He'd thought he'd been sharing a cell with a transport pilot. Finding out Daior was actually a really expensive, really specialised, mercenary? That drew some unpleasant possibilities to the fore. An Advanced Tek was like the equivalent of three soldiers. From a special forces unit. He flashed back to an earlier conversation. X-rays. Mainframes.

Terran's heart rate sped up as he put two and two together and came out with a very explosive four.

Until then, Terran had been assuming he'd been grabbed because of *who* he was. All modesty aside, he was worth quite a bit in ransom money. Could possibly be used for leverage against certain people. But if they'd grabbed him because of *what* he was?

"I need to get out of here," Terran told Daior. "Now."

"Why now?"

"Because if you're an Advanced Tek, then I think I know why they want me. And it's not good."

Daior must have heard the urgency in Terran's voice, because his eyes hardened. "Want to share?"

Maybe Daior was right about the camera's lack of audio. But maybe he wasn't. Either way, Terran couldn't take the risk.

"Not here," he replied. "Just know they'll take me apart and...and they probably won't put me back together."

"Not good enough."

Daior suddenly seemed to realise he was still holding Terran on his lap. Terran found himself abruptly dumped back on the floor.

Dai surged to his feet, muttering under his breath. "You're not going to tell me, are you?" he asked between curses.

That really wasn't what Terran had been expecting to hear. Nor was Dai's tone of resignation. With the way Dai had pushed him away, Terran had been expecting anger. Annoyance. Frustration. All the emotions that Terran was, apparently, extremely good at inducing in others. But Daior giving in? Terran had been gearing up for a lot more argument, first.

Daior eyed Terran with an unfathomable expression. "The instant we're out of here, I expect a full confession," he warned.

Terran nodded. "You deserve it."

Besides that, Terran wasn't quite ready to give up on starting something with his new mercenary friend. Best not to dive headfirst into a potential relationship with huge secrets between them. Particularly ones like Terran's.

"Block the camera for me, would you?" Dai was already moving as he asked the question, crossing the small cell in a few determined strides.

Terran followed orders, although he wasn't certain how effective he was. The camera was pretty high up and Terran wasn't exactly tall. He managed at least to get in the way, though, to keep Daior's hands out of sight.

Terran watched in fascination, completely impressed with how fast Daior worked. It took Dai less than a minute and a half to pop open the lock.

Daior shrugged at Terran's wide-eyed stare. "The inner locks are easy," he said self-consciously. "It's the outer ones that are stubborn bitches. The door will lock behind me, so just stay put."

"Wait. What? I thought—"

"Still no way off the planet," Daior reiterated impatiently. "I'm going to try, again, to find the blasted Comm Centre."

"The camera," Terran protested. "Wouldn't it be better to make a run for it?"

"No. And they turned it off again."

Terran looked back and, sure enough, the red light had vanished. *Huh. So far? Not impressed with these guys.*

"I'm not going to sit here forever," Terran pointed out.

"I'll shut off the power if I find something," Dai told him. "The lock will automatically disengage. Straight down the hall, third corridor, turn left. That's the easiest door to break out of. Of course, this all assumes I'll actually find the Comm Centre. Which I doubt. Didn't find it the first three recons, can't imagine I will this time, either."

"If you don't find it?"

"Then I'll be back. You *stay put.*"

Terran was usually really good about ignoring orders like that, but Daior's expression promised really nasty consequences, so he nodded. Terran watched Daior slip through the door after one last, admonishing glare. He had every intention of obeying Dai's orders.

At least, for a little while.

# Chapter Three

"Gods take it." Richard snarled the words, letting his fist land heavily on the table in front of him.

Ensign Edwards jumped. Richard glared at him until the man's face went even more pasty white than usual.

"S-sorry, sir," the frightened man stuttered.

Richard glared some more.

"Thank you, Ensign. You're dismissed." Layna's deep, throaty voice made Edwards jump again. Richard's lieutenant waited until the beleaguered junior officer had scrambled from the room before speaking again.

"You shouldn't frighten the young ones," she said dryly. "It has a remarkably distressing effect on crew morale."

Richard would have snarled at Layna, too, but knew it was a waste of energy. It was why the woman was his second in command, after all. She was absolutely fearless.

Of course, the fact she'd been his best friend since primary school helped, too.

Layna put a hand to her ear, murmuring something brief into her communication implant. For about the millionth time, Richard wished he had one of those. He hated not knowing what was going on. But he was Altaireon nobility. Getting technological enhancements was something that just wasn't done. Things like that were saved for the army and merchants.

There were many days when Richard wished he was either one. Usually on days, like today, when his brother was busy turning his life upside down. Again.

Layna slid into the chair next to Richard and patted his arm. She probably meant it as a sympathetic move, but if that were the case, she should try to do a better job of hiding the expression in her eyes. Amusement, at his expense, no less, didn't exactly convey sympathy.

"I'm sure Terran is just wandering around, completely distracted, with no idea how late it is," Layna said.

Richard rubbed his forehead, feeling a headache building. A headache always seemed to build whenever his brother entered the conversation.

"You mean he's off trying to get laid by as many strangers as possible," Richard corrected. "Lord knows what goes through that boy's head."

Layna shrugged. "Hey, at least he keeps current on his vaccinations and won't come back sick. That's one less worry."

Richard glared, not even bothering to say the words.

"Right," Layna said with a nod. "Not helping."

An awkward silence fell over the room, dragging longer as Richard stared out of the large window at the glittering expanse of stars. For once, the *Celsius* wasn't moving, affording him a rare opportunity just to look at the strange beauty of space. Despite travelling the galaxies for more years than he cared to contemplate, it was a sight of which he never tired. So massive, yet so familiar, his little corner of the universe.

Richard was Altaireon's Diplomatic Consul. As such, he spent his time making his rounds of all the planets with which Altaireon held trade agreements and political alliances. And Altaireon was a powerful planet, meaning there were many. He loved it, meeting with people, navigating the often treacherous waters of politics. And then, of course, there was the odd side job for the Naturide Federation.

According to legend, the Naturide Federation had its origins in an organisation from Earth, Interpol. As Earth had expanded and colonised suitable planets, the new settlements had formed their own governments and social structures. But with so many people scattered over such a vast area, some form of regulation had become necessary to preserve human rights. Once a simple investigative force, the Naturide Federation had evolved into a combination law enforcement, medical and rescue team and military force. They kept interplanetary conflicts from exploding into all-out war.

And, on occasion, they recruited men like Richard, who had widespread contacts, into procuring information for them. It fed that well-hidden side of him, the one that Terran would swear didn't exist. The part that thrived on intrigue and adrenaline.

Layna tapped her fingers irritably on the table, scowling at whatever she was being told.

"Still no sign of him?" Richard asked.

"Nothing. He missed the last shuttle back. No messages, no contact, no sightings."

And that wasn't like Terran. Oh, he disappeared frequently. But usually he called in to tell them he was disappearing.

There had been no 'I'm going off for a few days, see you soon' messages. Which concerned Richard. A lot.

"He'll turn up," Layna assured him. "He always does."

"I just can't shake the feeling of impending doom," Richard drawled. "I've learnt to heed that feeling."

"Edwards says they last saw him on Mackenzie Street, going into one of those flashy, neon sign-coated strip joints," Layna said.

"I know."

"They checked all up and down the entertainment district, and he wasn't in any of his usual haunts."

"I heard that part, too."

"And—"

"You really don't need to repeat the entire report to me. I was standing right next to you." Richard ground his teeth together and reminded himself that Layna was really, really good at her job. Therefore, he shouldn't fire her. And she was a girl, so he couldn't hit her, either.

"Relax," Layna said. "I have the geek patrol scanning security tapes from the entire town. We'll find him."

"If my father heard you call his hand-picked technology crew the 'geek patrol', he'd have your hide," Richard felt compelled to point out.

"Well, good thing he's not here, then," came the chipper reply.

Richard let the familiar banter distract him and opened his mouth for another retort. Layna's upraised hand stopped him.

"Right. Patch it through."

The expression on Layna's face went from teasing to grim in a nanosecond, and Richard's stomach knotted up with tension.

"Something happened to him," he stated.

"The video feed is on its way right now."

The conference room was rarely used, but it was extremely well-equipped. The long, gleaming table was designed to intimidate, along with seating an obscene number of people. The stoic, forbidding air of the shining walls and the cold atmosphere made the room anything but comfortable.

It was where Richard came to escape. Not because he liked the blasted place, but because people were usually reluctant to bother him in here. He wasn't the only person to find the room over-the-top, ostentatious and cold.

The gleaming wood surface of the table reflected his sour expression with far too much accuracy. That expression was appearing more and more often of late, and he didn't like it. Richard pushed the button on his right side, glad when a section of the tabletop slid aside and marred the image. A small control panel gave him access to the audio-visual components, and he punched up the code for the video feed. The round ball that rose from the centre of the table projected an image on all sides, enabling anyone at the long table to watch.

Richard narrowed his eyes and considered moving to another room. From the far end where he sat, the screen looked damn small. But moving was too much effort, and he needed to know what sort of trouble his blasted brother had found this time.

"What the hell does he think he's doing?" Richard growled as a very familiar figure paused on a crowded sidewalk, looked around then entered a building through a pair of battered doors.

"Offhand," Layna commented, "I'd say you were right earlier, and he's looking to get laid."

"Not helping, Lieutenant."

"Didn't think it was, Richie."

The video flashed into fast forward, stopping when Terran exited the same doors. An extremely satisfied smirk covered his delicate features as he started walking down the street. The pavement teemed with people, even at the late hour. Richard kept losing sight of Terran among the crowd and behind the bulky forms of passing vehicles. Quentain was a land-rich planet, the towns spreading out instead of up. The place always made Richard claustrophobic, though. Buildings pressed close together, traffic clogged paved streets.

The crowd thinned as Terran left behind the flashing neon of the entertainment district and moved into the far quieter commercial district. The storefronts were dark at that time of night, although the street lamps still shone brightly on the cracked pavement.

Terran paused and cocked his head, looking around. He took a few steps down a side-street, biting his lip, glancing over his shoulder. Clearly debating whether he was ready to return to the docks and the waiting shuttle.

"I'm going to ground him for the rest of eternity," Richard commented, watching Terran's indecision. If the little brat had disappeared just to grab some more sex…

"Good luck with that. Hold up." Layna's teasing tone dropped away again and she sat forward.

A man came into view, blocking Terran's path and waving his hand in a question.

"This thing got sound?" Richard asked.

Layna shook her head.

"Remind me to donate money to the city's security force so they can upgrade their cameras."

"What, you want to see *and* hear your brother's high-jinxes?"

"Scratch the donation."

The man spoke again and Terran turned, pointing down the street.

That was when the two additional men leapt from the shadows. One grabbed Terran's elbow and another moved behind him. An instant later, Terran went limp.

Richard roared a really nasty curse that would have had his mother screeching at him. The small group disappeared into the heavy shadows between a drugstore and a pub, Terran draped over the largest one's shoulder.

"Layna—"

"On it, Captain." Layna ran from the room, snapping commands into her Comm with rapid skill.

"Damn you, Terran, what have you got yourself into now?"

Richard shut off the video and shoved his chair back. He had a long, long list of things demanding his attention. All of which had just been dumped aside in favour of rescuing his brother.

Again.

Richard headed for the bridge wondering, for the thousandth time, what he had done in his previous life to get dealt such a shitty hand in this one.

Chaos reigned on the bridge, officers and pilots milling around in confused circles. Disrupt one little bit of their flight plan, and the whole place got sucked down a black hole.

Richard stood inside the doors, surveying the frantic—and mostly pointless—activity. Then he cleared his throat.

Instant silence greeted him. Ah, but it was good to be in charge.

"We have a little change in plans," he said grimly. "It seems Terran has managed to get himself kidnapped. I have a trace out trying to locate him. In the meantime, we're remaining in stationary orbit until we get a heading."

A pilot raised his hand tentatively. What were they, in school? Richard bit back the snarky comment and waved at the man.

"Sir, what about the Galactrician Council meeting?"

Richard bit back a curse, having completely forgotten about that. Galactricians had vicious tempers. They weren't going to be happy about him missing the biannual Council meeting, which usually hashed out conflicts and agreements from all three planets under the Galactricians' rule. Well, they'd just have to get along without him this time. If they didn't like it, they could take it up with the regent. Damien, regent and current ruler of Altaireon, was an old friend. And he would be the first one to tell Richard to scratch the meeting and track down Terran.

"I'll contact the Council and let them know I won't be attending. All other meetings will also be put on hold until further notice. Our first—our only—priority is getting Terran back. Understood?"

"Yes, sir."

The barked agreement came from all corners of the large room and Richard nodded in satisfaction.

"Good. Everyone can clear out, but all personnel are on emergency standby. Trixel, make the announcement."

"Yes, sir."

His perky communications expert trotted off and the rest of the crew quickly followed.

"Are you sure that was wise?"

Richard sighed, not needing to turn to see the owner of that familiar voice. He knew exactly what expression would be covering Jackson's stern features—a mixture of disapproval and deference.

The disapproval Richard bought. The deference was just an act. They'd known each other far too long for that.

"Terran comes first, you know that," Richard replied.

"Yes, but nothing says you need to go retrieve him yourself. There are plenty of law enforcement—"

"I'm not bringing them into this," Richard snapped.

"Sir—"

"No."

On this point, Richard wasn't going to budge.

Jackson cleared his throat and stared fixedly at Richard, eyes averted just enough to remain inside the boundaries of rank.

"I'll alert some of my contacts at the Federation," Richard finally conceded. "Those I know I can trust to keep the situation quiet."

Jackson opened his mouth and Richard cut him off with a quick slash of his hand.

"That's all I can I do. We don't know what we'll find and I won't risk Terran's safety any further."

Jackson gave in, albeit with visible reluctance. "Very well. But I suggest you contact your father immediately."

After imparting that incredibly unwelcome reminder, Jackson followed the rest of the crew and made himself scarce. Richard found himself alone on the bridge.

He dropped into his chair, sighing. He ran one hand through his hair, tugging in irritation at the short strands. He blankly gazed out at the fathomless depths of space.

All the balls were rolling, all activities in motion. All but one. Jackson had been right about that, but it wasn't going to be easy.

Richard had to call his dad and let him know that Richard had lost Terran.

Again.

# Chapter Four

Daior didn't think Terran was quite human. Oh, he certainly looked the part, but humans, in general, didn't purr. At the very least, there was something funky going on with Terran's DNA.

Daior contemplated what that something might be as he slipped down one empty hall after another, steadily making his way back to the more familiar areas of the complex and their cell. The nape of his neck itched and he had this nearly overwhelming urge to get back to Terran, now. It was an effort, keeping his feet at a steady pace.

The lack of activity was really starting to bug him. Where *was* everyone? It wasn't even mid-afternoon, yet. If Daior didn't know better, he would swear the place was abandoned, just him and Terran. But he did know better, which brought up all kinds of questions. He knew that whoever was running the place was relying more heavily on technology and security systems than actual bodies, but still. Daior knew for a fact there were at least a dozen guards wandering around somewhere, not to mention the medical and administrative personnel. He'd steered clear of any areas where the latter two groups might be, but he should have run into at least one guard.

Daior didn't know whether to be relieved or not when he finally reached the all too familiar cell door without incident. He tripped the lock and slid back inside, casting one last look around at the still-empty hallway.

"All clear," he announced. "I think I actually found the damn Comm Centre this time. It's tucked back in what looks like a janitor's closet from the outside, but no closet I've ever seen has a lock like that. I'm good, but even I couldn't cra—"

Daior blinked, suddenly realising he was talking to an empty room. He even crossed their small, cave-like cell and peered into what Terran derisively called the 'toilet closet'. Nothing. The only sign that Terran had ever been there was the scattered remains of their aborted board game.

"Fuck!" His curse echoed off the stone.

Daior hovered uncertainly in front of the door, debating whether or not to charge back out and go looking for Terran. But if he did, and Terran came back... Daior had been lucky last time out, what with the lack of contact with unfamiliar, warm bodies. No guarantee the halls would stay clear, though. And if he got caught, chances were they'd stick Terran and Daior in separate cells. That just wouldn't do, particularly if Terran were still set on making some sort of escape attempt. Which Daior knew he was.

He rubbed his forehead, shoving his hands into his hair, tangling his fingers in the dark, unruly strands.

All right, so it probably wasn't the best idea to go roaming the halls again. The place was a damn maze, all winding steel hallways and tiny rooms. A thorough search would take hours. Best to wait, at least for a while.

An hour later, food arrived. Dai ignored it. *Where was Terran?*

Two hours later, and Daior was still waiting. The scenarios running through his head were about to drive him nuts. He was on the verge of giving up, going hunting.

The sound of male laughter filtered through from the narrow hallway outside. Muscles tensing, Daior watched the steel door. It banged open forcefully, and in stumbled Terran.

Daior growled, low and vicious, wanting to launch himself past the kid and start swinging. The light shone off smooth skin as the kid wrapped his arms around a naked stomach. The door clanged shut and locked again before Daior could move. Footsteps faded before he managed to unstick his feet and take a step towards Terran. Terran stumbled back, shaking, until he hit the door.

"Easy," Daior soothed. "It's just me."

"Sorry," Terran mumbled to his feet. He still hugged himself tightly, slender body trembling. "You find anything while you were out?"

Daior ignored the question. "Did they hurt you?"

Terran shook his head, but Daior wasn't sure he bought it. He backed off, though, taking his usual seat on the ground. After a slight pause, Terran perched himself atop his rock, breathing hard, breath catching every few seconds.

*Oh, damn.*

"You sure you're okay?"

"Yeah."

But Daior heard a small sniffle.

*Damn, again.*

"Come here, kid," Daior encouraged with his best gentle smile. It wasn't an expression he was all that used to. "You must be freezing."

Terran bit into his lower lip with even, white teeth and peered up through blue eyes from underneath long lashes. Then, as if losing some inner battle, the slim figure flung himself across the empty space. Slightly chilled skin landed in Daior's arms as Terran practically tried to crawl into him. The smaller man kept apologising even as he wrapped his arms around Daior's neck and clung tightly.

"Sorry," Terran said again. "You never said. Did you find anything?"

*Distraction. Okay, good.* That Daior could do. Comforting? Not so much.

"I think I might have found where they've stashed the Comm. Centre. I didn't have enough time to break in, not with that lock. I wanted to get back before they noticed I was missing. Speaking of, I imagine they weren't happy when they came for you and I wasn't here."

Terran shook his head. "I don't think they paid any attention. I was near the door, and they just grabbed and went. Guess they thought you were in the back or something."

"These guys?" Daior muttered. "Clearly not the best money can buy. Weird. Top-notch facility like this, you would think they could afford better employees."

He held Terran in silence until the worst of the shivers subsided.

"Feeling better?" he asked when the smaller man finally lay quiet in his arms.

"A little," Terran replied.

"You want to tell me what happened?"

"Not really."

"You will anyway," Daior stated.

"Yeah, I guess I will."

The tiny smile accompanying the words shouldn't make Daior feel so good, but there it was. Made no sense to him, but then again, he wasn't exactly the analytical type.

"They didn't hurt me," Terran continued. "But…it's coming, you know? They hauled me to the med ward, ran preliminary tests. Blood work and scans, the whole works. The doctor was really happy."

"Woulda scared me, too," Daior mumbled. That doctor was about as creepy as they came. Tall and gangly with wild eyes. The bastard had way too much in common with those old movie mad scientists. Daior hadn't been able to resist heckling the guy for adhering so strictly to stereotypes. Of course, typical of said stereotypes, Daior hadn't been able to get any reaction. No sense of humour, that one.

"So what happened to your clothes?" Daior asked.

"The stupid guards wouldn't give them back after the exam. And they kept staring."

Daior didn't like the sound of that. He growled low, mind busy running through a litany of curses.

Terran patted his chest, now trying to soothe Daior. "We can get out of the cell," he pointed out. "And if you've found a way to get word to someone, we can get a ship in here."

"I don't know if any of my contacts are close enough."

"My brother probably is. We can call him. Not sure I want to be rescued by Richard again, but it's better than the alternative."

"And what exactly is the alternative?" Daior asked. He could make a pretty good guess, but he wanted Terran to spell it out.

"I'm…different," Terran admitted softly. "My DNA. I'm not like everyone else, not put together like everyone else. I imagine whoever is funding this operation wants to study me. I just get the feeling their method of study isn't going to be very good for my long-term health."

Daior hummed in thought. "No, I imagine it won't be. I figured it would be something along those lines."

"What about you?" Terran interjected. "Won't they pull you apart, too? Come to that, why haven't they already?"

"Probably because they can't find anything unusual about me," Daior replied calmly. "My systems are extremely well integrated. Most of my technological enhancements were added when I was a child."

"Isn't that illegal?" Terran's nose wrinkled, and he looked a little disgusted.

"Very," Daior replied. "But like these guys, the scientists who created me weren't too concerned with legality. The upshot is, though, when turned off, my enhancements are pretty much invisible. I honestly have no idea why they haven't killed me yet, but I won't complain too much."

Not that the guards would find him easy to kill. No, if it had come to that, Daior would have made a break for the frontier, carnivorous beasts be damned. But he would *not* have been pleased at being forced to tramp through jungle and wilderness. Daior just wasn't the outdoors type. At all. He'd spent most of his life in space or on the central planets, where people had the money needed to pay for his services. He'd never been camping and didn't really want to change that.

Terran sighed and cuddled closer, resting more of his weight on Daior's chest. "I really just want to go somewhere safe," he said.

"Not home?" Daior questioned.

Terran shook his head, a hint of his usual, sunny smile peeking out. "No, because if I went home, I wouldn't get to keep you."

"Oh, you're keeping me, are you?"

"Absolutely."

Daior settled Terran more firmly in his lap, pulling Terran sideways and stroking his thumb absently over Terran's sharp hip bone. "Don't I get a say in this?"

"Nope," Terran announced. "If I left it up to you, nothing would ever happen."

"What can I say? Ambition isn't really my thing."

"I'm not talking ambition. I'm talking about letting loose enough. We're both attracted to each other, stuck together with nothing to do, and I'm more than willing. You, however, have not once taken advantage of the situation. And I want you to. Take advantage, that is."

Daior chuckled. "Kid, believe me, it has nothing to do with not wanting you. I just don't feel this is the time or place to get distracted by sex."

Terran stroked Daior's chest. Daior didn't think the smaller man even realised he was doing it.

"I really doubt they'll come back tonight," Terran pointed out. "So it wouldn't matter if you got a bit...distracted."

Daior hummed again, leaning down, inhaling the scent of male and lemons. How the kid still smelt so good, even after so much time locked up, was a mystery to Daior. Here he was, the hairy woodsman, and Terran didn't even have a five o'clock shadow.

"I should really go take another look at that lock," Daior mused, the words not really registering as he ran his hand over Terran's light, silky hair.

"Later," Terran murmured.

He wrapped his hands around Daior's neck and pulled their heads together. Their mouths clashed, and Terran didn't waste any time, plunging his tongue deep into the recesses of Daior's mouth. Terran's knees dropped to rest on either side of Daior's outstretched legs. He rose up until he found the right angle. Hot, moist, rough. The ferociousness of the kiss contrasted marvellously with the softness of Terran's busy tongue, those pretty lips.

"Wait," Daior gasped, not really meaning it but not liking the feeling of the world tipping on its side and spinning out of control.

"No."

"I thought what happened earlier was for…" Daior let the sentence trail off, tilting his head ever so slightly in a suggestive gesture towards their electronic voyeur. The thought of that, of the way Terran had used that kiss, almost had him shoving Terran aside. Almost.

Terran shook his head emphatically and something inside Daior relaxed and unwound.

"I want you," Terran said. "I have since the first minute I saw you. The camera was just a nice excuse to touch."

The way he kissed Daior again demonstrated just how much he wanted him.

Dai stopped arguing. He knew when he was being an idiot. He wanted Terran, Terran wanted him. They were, for the moment, safe. Another reconnaissance run probably wouldn't be the wisest move right now, with the guards at loose ends. Why the hell was he trying to talk Terran out of something they both wanted so badly?

Daior might not always be the brightest merc out there, but he wasn't a complete idiot. He pulled Terran back into another scorching kiss, roaming his hands over all that naked skin pressed to him.

"Someone's wearing too many clothes," Terran whispered, nipping at his ear. "And it's not me."

*Yeah, naked sounds fantastic.* But that would require letting go of Terran, and Daior wasn't quite ready to do that.

The choice was taken out of his hands as Terran began to slide down his chest. He growled a protest, a protest which cut off abruptly as Terran squeezed his cock with one hot hand, burning even through the fabric of his cargo pants.

Terran pressed his face against Dai's hip to hide his grin. Daior looked ready to go off, and Terran hadn't even got to the good parts yet. Terran worked down the zipper of Daior's pants, knuckles brushing against hard, hot skin. *Oh, happy day.* Dai went commando.

He ran his fingertips over the weeping head. *Oh, that feels so perfect.* Dai was big. Thick and hot and satiny. Terran could hardly wait to get that thick cock in his arse. It was going to feel so very good. And he needed it. Badly.

Terran wiggled Dai's pants down as far as he could and went straight for the good stuff. His lips closed over the red, engorged head, and he sucked. Hard.

Daior shouted, hips bucking. "Baby, hang on. I want—"

Terran pulled off with a small pop. "Me, too."

Daior growled, grasping Terran's hips and tossing him down, albeit with gentle care. Terran landed on his back, giggling madly. The giggle morphed into a moan as Dai tugged on his left nipple then laved the nub of flesh before gifting it with a sharp nip.

"Oh, do that again." Small bits of rock were digging into Terran's back, but he couldn't care less. "More, Dai. More. Please."

"Soon," Dai promised. "But I don't have anything. I don't want to hurt you. Have to get you ready for me, first."

Terran reached up, wrapped his hands in Dai's shaggy mop of dark hair and tugged forcibly. "I'm ready," he practically wailed.

Daior grinned. "Nah. You're nowhere near the exploding point yet, baby."

Daior covered Terran, his substantial bulk a surprisingly comforting feeling. Dai took his time exploring with lips and tongue, gripping firmly to keep Terran in place. The smell of arousal hung thick and heavy in the air, and Terran's pleading moans and needy whimpers filled the silence.

Daior moved lower, flicking out his tongue to taste Terran with a barely-felt motion. He moved up one hand to cup Terran's balls. Terran had rarely been more grateful for the lack of hair down there. The feeling of those large, calloused hands on his bare skin was marvellous.

"Damn," Daior said, running his fingertip from the base to the tip of Terran's aching cock. "That's pretty."

"I don't care how it looks, just do something with it!"

Dai smirked. "You need to learn patience, baby. And I think I'm just the man to teach you."

"If you don't move in the next four seconds I'll—" The words ended in a deep groan when Daior squeezed Terran's balls in one large palm. That was okay. Terran wouldn't have been able to think up a decent threat, anyway. Not with Daior's hands on him.

Despite his near desperate pleading, when Dai finally acted, it caught Terran by surprise. In one swift move, Dai pulled Terran's legs over his shoulders and dived down. He paid brief homage to Terran's cock with his tongue then moved on to his balls before painting a slow circle around Terran's hole.

"Dai!"

Terran arched as best he could, throwing his head back as lightning ripped up his spine. His chest was tight, lack of air making him dizzy. Rocks dug into his flesh, adding a delicious sting to the painful pleasure. *Damn.* Nothing had ever felt so amazing as Dai's tongue rimming his arse.

Dai added his hand to the busy activity of his tongue. Terran writhed and bucked as Daior continued to work Terran's sphincter muscle open with spit-coated fingers. The pleasure was so intense, it kept edging over into pain, and Terran couldn't decide if he wanted to get closer or yank away so he could breathe.

Daior didn't give Terran a choice, keeping him pinned in place while he mercilessly played Terran's body like a well-tuned instrument.

Terran was nearly screaming Daior's name by the time the bigger man pulled three fingers free of his arse. The tight ring of muscle clenched briefly, as if unwilling to give up the captive causing so much pleasure. Daior pressed another long kiss to his crease, working a bit more spit inside with his tongue, before shifting his weight and running his tongue along Terran's thighs.

"Ready, baby?" he asked.

"Now, now. For the love of the stars, Dai!"

With jaw-dropping strength, Daior flipped Terran over.

"Gonna be rough," Daior panted in explanation.

Terran braced himself on his hands and knees, pushing backwards until the head of Daior's cock brushed against his hole. Daior used the pre-cum dripping liberally from his own cock as lubrication then balanced himself on one arm, using the other hand to guide himself into Terran.

Terran's body welcomed Dai's cock like a missing part. Only the briefest resistance slowed his entrance, with only the slightest pinch of pain for Terran.

"Terran!" Daior plunged deep in one smooth stroke.

He bottomed out, the hair around his groin brushing against Terran's smooth skin. It sent the most delicious ripples up Terran's spine. Terran was babbling, and he knew it, but he couldn't remember sex ever feeling like this. Each stroke in and out nailed his prostate as if connected by a string. Terran's muscles were jerking, body shaking, as Dai drove him higher than he could ever remember flying. Terran dropped onto his forearms, bracing himself more firmly and shoving his arse up and out.

"Please, please, please."

Terran was barely aware of his chanting words. Daior groaned, the sound beautiful and arousing and oh, so sexy. Terran squeezed with his lower body, determined to send Daior as high as the big man was sending him.

"Gods, baby, you feel so good. Tight and perfect. Just a little more…"

Daior curved over Terran's back, wrapping him in molten heat. Terran felt surrounded, consumed, completely owned by the man moving in and out with a steady rhythm.

Terran's release crashed over him without warning. He arched, nearly throwing Dai off-balance, screaming curses at the top of his lungs as his vision faded in and out. His body rocked with tremors, as if someone had set off a series of firecrackers in his gut. The pleasure seemed endless, washing over him in wave upon wave. Still Daior kept moving, the constant drag on Terran's prostate prolonging his orgasm until Terran thought his body might fly apart. He was just going to break into tiny pieces of gooey, pleasure-soaked Terran, he knew it.

He pushed back into Daior's welcoming body, riding through the intense sensations. Daior growled low in his throat, the sound almost painful in its rough friction.

Daior's control finally broke. He roared loudly as heat flooded Terran.

"Oh, holy—" Terran broke off in astonishment as Daior's release triggered a second orgasm. Terran was far too exhausted to do anything but let it wash through him.

Daior's strong arms gave out with the last of his seed, and he collapsed. Even then, Dai tried to look out for Terran, turning them so Terran wasn't crushed. Terran rolled, sprawling so he could toss one arm over his lover's hard, muscled chest. He followed it with one leg until he lay half on top of his new lover like a living, breathing blanket. Terran squirmed until he found just the right spot before relaxing with a sigh.

Daior didn't seem inclined to move him. In fact, the man wrapped one thick forearm around him and pulled him closer. Their skin threatened to meld together permanently, both of them sticky with sweat and semen.

Terran was absolutely, positively thrilled at the satisfied smile splitting Daior's scruffy beard and lightening his craggy features. He found he was smiling, too, a big, happy grin against sweaty skin. *Oh, yeah.* He could stay here for a few hours. Days. Months, even.

It occurred to him vaguely that it wasn't possible, that they should be moving, doing something. But he was really far too tired and sated to worry about much of anything. Not for quite a while.

Terran sleepily patted the thickly muscled side. "You did good."

Daior's deep laugh rumbled comfortably through Terran's pleasure-drugged body. The sexy sound followed him into a contented sleep.

# Chapter Five

Terran woke still sprawled on top of Daior—or at least, halfway on top. Terran tended to wiggle in his sleep. He liked cuddling up to the big guy, though. Maybe too much. Terran was already falling hard for the cranky mercenary. Not the most ideal conditions, obviously, but it seemed inevitable just the same. Almost like fate, although Dai would probably scoff if Terran used that word.

So would Richard, Terran thought with a wince. He could just imagine the scene if he tried to bring Daior home to meet his big brother. Richard would throw ten kinds of fits, insist it was all physical, that Terran had just, as usual, felt horny.

There would be some basis to that accusation, too. Terran would be the first to admit to living up to the tomcat, overly-sexed, gay male stereotype. He liked sex, liked to spread the love.

But that didn't mean he would ignore a good thing when he found it, and Dai was promising to be a very good thing, indeed. Terran's admittedly voracious sexual appetite meant he'd spent more time than was probably wise flitting from club to club. Richard had commented more than once that it was a good thing vaccines had made STDs a thing of the past. Usually, Terran had scratched his itch and moved on, the men—and occasionally women, if he had been desperate enough—leaving his thoughts as quickly as they had left his sights.

But all along, Terran had been looking. Richard didn't believe it, but Terran really wanted someone just for him, someone to cuddle up with at night once the itch had been satisfied. The string of one-night-stands littering his past merely served as stand-ins until he could find that someone.

And if that someone ended up being Daior? All the better. Because he could really, really see himself cuddling with the big man for a long time. Heck, even the mere thought made him purr with happiness.

Daior grunted and moved his arm. "Shh," he murmured, not really awake. "Sleeping, Tam."

*Oh, no, he did not.*

Terran sat up, indignant, but the motion made his stomach pitch, the sudden cramp and rising nausea catching him completely off guard. Terran's hand shot up to cover his mouth as he gagged.

*Oh, stars. Not now.* Terran's spine began to itch, and a small, pained mewl escaped his clamped lips. He knew from past experience that the cramping and aching would grow and grow until the pain was all he could feel, all on which he could concentrate.

Terran took his hand away from his mouth and rubbed at his abdomen, trying in vain to massage away the ache. Exhaustion tried to pull him back into sleep, but he fought it.

It took effort, but he dragged himself off Daior and slid to the floor. He really didn't want to wake Daior. The questions would start then, and he was in no shape to deal with them.

Terran curled up in a small ball on the chilled stone, wrapping his arms around his middle. His gut continued to churn and he could taste bile in his mouth. He swallowed it down, another whimper breaking free.

A few feet away, Daior shifted and muttered, grumbling inaudibly to himself as he rolled over. Terran stared through blurry eyes and bit his lip, wanting desperately to wake up the bigger man and just…be held.

But he didn't. Instead, he tucked his head close to his chest, curling tighter into a small circle, one that no human should really be able to manage.

Then he let his eyes slide shut and prayed he and Dai would get out of there soon. Before it was too late.

* * * *

Daior woke to the dulcet tones of someone retching out their guts on the floor. *Shit.* He blinked his eyes a few times, trying to get his thoughts working. He hadn't intended to go to sleep. With their captors being more active, he had intended to make another try at the Comm Centre as soon as he thought it would be safe.

*Wait. Retching. Shit.* Daior rolled over, back protesting loudly. Terran was curled up in the corner, hurling like he was dying.

"Terran, you feeling all right?" *Okay, stupid question. Blame it on the sleepies.* His mind wasn't working at full capacity just yet.

Terran rested his forehead on his arms, breathing heavily, before he started another round.

Dai rose to his knees and put one hand on Terran's shoulder. The smaller man was shaking, shudders racking his thin frame. "Terran?"

Terran gasped something. Daior leaned close to try to make out the words, but at that moment the door flew open.

Terran turned terror-filled eyes Daior's way, and Dai knew they had run out of time.

With a low growl, Daior launched himself at the nearest figure. They tumbled to the floor, Dai slamming his elbow into the soft flesh of the guard's abdomen on the way down. A quick knee to the groin, and he moved on to the next target.

"Daior!"

*Shit.* One of the uniformed men had Terran out in the hallway. Terran was struggling, hissing and spitting madly, but he was no match for the much larger man holding him tightly. Daior dropped his weight and spun, knocking the second man's legs out from under him. Dai made it a few feet in Terran's direction before steely arms grabbed, pinning Dai's elbows tightly to his side. Daior kicked backwards, throwing his weight into his attacker, trying to use his own mass to throw them off balance.

The guy was good. He braced himself, and Daior hit the ground. Hard.

"Will someone help me out here?" the guard yelled into Daior's ear.

Daior snarled and bucked. *Ah, fuck.* There was no help for it.

He slammed his head back. Sharp, stabbing pain and the sound of cracking bone, and Dai knew he'd hit his mark. The arms loosened, and Dai squirmed free, kicking the bleeding guard aside.

Dai staggered to his feet. Yeah, he'd done a number on the guard's face. Of course, now his head hurt like hell.

It wasn't until Daior's vision cleared that he realised he was alone in the room with two unconscious security personnel. Terran was nowhere to be found.

Daior cursed, kicking one of the prone bodies in frustration. He ran his hand through his tangled curls, mind racing.

Unfortunately, the conclusion was pretty obvious. Daior wasn't going to be much use to Terran right now. He was unarmed, on his own, no working enhancements.

*Damn it. Damn it. Exploding stars and planets. Curse it to the eighth dimension, wherever the fuck that is.* Dai had held out for ten damn years. Ten years of pretending to be normal. Ten years on his own. Now, within the space of a few days, one short, skinny man had changed everything.

Daior wasn't really the philosophical type. He wasn't going to start dissecting his motivations. He was just going to grit his teeth and break every vow he'd ever made to himself.

Simple enough.

Daior yanked on his clothing with jerky motions. He rolled over one of the guards and started searching through the unconscious man's pockets, muttering to himself. "When I find the bastard who started all this,

I swear I'll—You throw up on my foot and I'll break your neck," he told the gagging man. A swift fist to the jaw, and Dai was dealing with a limp body again. He finished rummaging and moved on to the next man.

"It's about damn time," he said in satisfaction, fishing out a ring of key cards. *Finally.* He'd been way overdue for some good luck. Now, if it would just hold a bit longer, maybe he could get himself and Terran out of this damn mess.

He made rapid progress through the bowels of the facility. The halls were cold, crude remnants of an old building. Within minutes, he shoved open the door separating the original structure from the new additions. Here, steel gleamed and the air tickled his nostrils with the tang of ozone from a high-end, efficient air processing unit.

Daior hummed under his breath, trying to remember which corridor led where. The next door he encountered was locked, so he dug the cards out of his pocket and started swiping them across the access pad. He was shuffling though them, on try number three, when the door slid open.

A skinny, brown-haired man in a white lab coat stared with an open mouth at Daior.

Daior grinned. "Hi, there."

"Um, hi?"

Daior yanked the clipboard out of the man's hands and whacked him over the head with it. He pulled the body through the door and locked it again before continuing on.

Twice Daior had to duck into empty rooms and wait for people to pass. What was up with this place?

Before it had been empty, deserted. Now there were people crawling all over.

It seemed to take an eternity before Daior stood in front of the door he'd come across the day before. He ran through the key cards rapidly, keeping one eye on his surroundings. The room sat at the edge of what appeared to be the main administrative area, and Dai figured someone would be coming along soon.

As if in answer to his thought, low voices bounced off the walls. Daior cursed under his breath. The sound almost drowned out the small snick as the lock disengaged. He had the door shoved open before the light could even blink green.

Shut inside the cold room, Daior took a deep breath. He made sure to seal the door, keeping out any unwanted visitors. Three long strides and he stood in front of a massive bank of monitors.

High tech in here, all the way. It actually took Daior a few minutes to puzzle out the various controls. He pulled up one of the swivel chairs lining the counter and dropped into it. The system hummed cheerfully as it fired up. After that, it was a simple enough matter to dial in the familiar frequency.

Now if only Tam hadn't changed his personal frequency and was within range…

Daior stared at the fuzzy screen, tapping his fingers against the plastic table in impatience. "Tam?" he asked. "You there?"

*Shit.* He checked his connections again, but everything blinked away happily. Gods, he always felt so stupid doing this, talking away to a blank screen. This was an advanced enough technology system that he should be good for at least two galaxies—thank the Gods huge breakthroughs had been made in instantaneous transmission in the last few years. Most of the major planets were within that distance, so Tam should be, too. Should be.

"Tam, you bastard, answer me," Dai snarled at the screen.

The picture flashed white, swirled around until Daior felt nauseous, then settled into place to reveal an achingly familiar face. Tamesis looked very much the same, although the closely-trimmed beard was a new addition. His pale blond hair was still long and caught back in its usual braid, and his ice blue eyes stared out from under heavy brows. There were new lines in the weathered face, cheekbones more pronounced, but it was, without a doubt, Daior's Tam.

"It's about time," Dai said. "I thought you were going to ignore me all day."

"Patient as always," Tam commented in his deep, husky voice. "I have to say, this is certainly a surprise. What was it you said? Not if the entire universe exploded into a burning inferno and I had the last container of ice? You always did have quite the way with words."

"Shut up."

"I thought you wanted me to talk. But I can go away." Tam's hand came into view, hovering over the off button.

"Jerk."

"Nice to see you, too."

Daior ground his teeth until his jaw popped. *Gods.* Ten years and the bastard was still as obnoxious as ever. If he had any other choice, Dai would cut the connection and forget the man even existed.

Unfortunately, he didn't have any other choice.

"I need your help," Dai spat out between clenched teeth. Damn, but that part had been harder than he'd thought it would be. Felt like he was trying to turn himself inside out, and the words wanted to lodge themselves in his throat.

Tam's brows drew low, lips pursing. "You're kidding, right?"

"Do I look like I'm kidding?"

"Not really, no. What kind of help?"

"I need an extraction."

"Who and where?"

"Me and my lover, Terran. And I don't know where, precisely."

The picture of the video link was extremely clear, enough so that Daior caught the brief flash of pain in Tam's eyes, the way the blue darkened. And what the hell was that about, anyway? Dai refused to feel guilty for moving on. He certainly didn't feel jealous at the thought of Tam with someone else. Just because he got irritable at the notion didn't mean anything. They had parted ways a long time ago. Unpleasantly, too.

"If you can leave this connection open, I've got the equipment to trace your location," Tam said. "What am I walking into?"

"Medical facility. Minimal security personnel. Lots of office staff, some doctors and nurses."

"So, an in-and-out."

"Should be."

Tam sighed, rubbing his hand along the back of his neck the way he always did when he was stressed. Dai kept his mouth shut as the silence stretched, knowing how his former partner worked. The man always thought things to death before he made any kind of decision.

"All right," Tam said. "I'll be there as soon as I can."

Daior nodded and turned off the video and audio, leaving enough power for Tam to follow. He just didn't need an audience for this next part.

The front of the communications room was set up with the actual communication equipment—monitors, speakers, tracking paraphernalia and a dozen other electronic devices that Daior couldn't actually name. There was a reason most people could only do the basics on this stuff. The rest was complicated enough so that most communications centres came equipped with a specialist.

The far side and back of the room contained the more common equipment. Computer systems for data entry, records, whatever else was needed. Daior knelt on the floor and yanked one of the towers out of its dock, checking the ports.

*Success.* He disconnected a few wires, connected up a few more.

Teks varied depending on where they had received their enhancements, but one thing remained the same. Their basic design generally consisted of technology laid over biology, computer chips hardwired into their brains. And, like any computer system, they required the occasional update or maintenance. Everything was done wirelessly, of course, but it required a hacker of above-average skill to get the job done.

Fortunately, Dai was above-average. It was, after all, programmed into him. It took him less than a minute to hack into the right system and find the necessary protocols to trigger a reboot in his dormant systems.

His finger hesitated for a long moment, each second ticking down, increasing the chance of discovery.

"Oh, just suck it up," Daior muttered to himself. Then he hit the 'Enter' button.

The shock of electricity hit him harder than he'd expected, sparks literally racing down his spine as his main CPU kicked in. His lungs tightened and his breathing shallowed as he rode the wave of pain as his systems rebooted for the first time in nearly a decade. Neon sparks shot across his vision and Daior closed his eyes tightly in a vain attempt to block them out. The flashing lights made him dizzy and more than a bit nauseous.

*Initialisation in sixty seconds.*

Daior hadn't heard that blasted feminine voice in a long, long time. Hadn't missed it, either. She was annoying as hell, always chirping some message inside his head.

When she started a monotone countdown, Daior wondered if this whole course of action were really necessary.

Then his vision disappeared into a white fuzz and a droning buzz underscored the words, *Initialisation begun.*

Daior's back arched in his chair, muscles seizing up. *Damn, that hurt.* His mind whirled as the augmentations tried to impose their will on his biology. He planted his feet on the floor, panting as information streamed into his head faster than his computer could process it. He writhed in place, fighting to regulate his system. Gods, this was why the docs had told him to pick one and stick, not switch his systems off and on. The technology overload was threatening to make his head burst.

Daior suddenly realised his lungs didn't feel so tight. Slowly, so slowly he almost didn't notice, the pain began to recede. He relaxed his muscles, gulping air, as the buzz dimmed.

*Initialisation complete.*

Daior sucked in air to his deprived lungs and rubbed his head. He stood, testing to make sure everything worked. He blinked a few times, took a couple of unsteady steps.

There it was. He had kind of missed this feeling. Closing his eyes, he mentally mapped out the compound around him.

Daior shook his head as his scan was interrupted a few times by fuzzy blips. It was probably going to take him months to get back to normal. Or whatever consisted normal for a technologically enhanced, genetically altered, whatever-the-hell he was.

But normal or not, the added boost would be enough to give him the immediate edge over any of the humans wandering around this place. He checked to make sure he still had the key cards on him.

*Good.* Tam should be on his way by now to get them the hell off this rock. In the meantime, Daior was going to go retrieve his little lover.

# Chapter Six

Terran heaved again, certain his guts were trying to come up through his nose. He clamped his mouth shut in a vain attempt at control. Wasn't like there was anything coming out of his stomach. Not anymore.

The man in the white coat made a small, fatherly sort of tsking sound. He patted Terran gently on the shoulder. "Easy there, young man. If you would stop fighting, I could give you something for that."

Terran yanked away from the touch sending cold chills up his spine. *Damn piranha.* Couldn't fool Terran with that nurturing act. He knew exactly what these men wanted, and it wasn't to protect and care for Terran, no matter what sort of nonsense they might spout. No, they wanted to poke and prod and splay him open, rip into his biology and find out what made him tick.

Terran wasn't feeling quite as resentful of his brother right now. Maybe he should have listened a little bit more when Richard had given him those lectures on the dangers rampant in space. About the people who would love nothing more than to take advantage of him or outright kill him.

He could practically hear Richard's voice in his head. *There are a lot of people out there who'll want you dead. They won't see you as human, just a half-breed abomination.*

Richard hadn't meant the words to hurt, although they had. For years, Terran had known full well his life would be in constant danger if anyone found out his DNA was so screwed up, mixed the way it was. But neither of them had foreseen anyone wanting to *study* him.

The lab door slid open with an almost silent hiss, admitting a second man wearing the standard white medical coat. Icy, pitiless eyes surveyed the bright, sterile room. He twisted his thin lips into a scowl, and Terran's stomach heaved again. He clamped his mouth shut again, canine teeth digging into his lower lip, chills running along his spine once more. This man, while outwardly very similar to the doctor who had been poking at Terran since the beginning, was much, much more dangerous.

"What the hell is taking so long, Emerson?" the new doctor snapped.

"It's a delicate—"

"The hell it is. Just strap the little freak down and get on with it. Our benefactor is growing impatient."

"I warned them this could take time," Emerson protested.

"You've had the subject for two days now and made absolutely no progress. I suggest you go and explain your lack of results to the Malkaians while I get started on the work you should have been doing."

Emerson scrambled out of the door with frantic haste. Terran had to choke back a plea for the man's return—Emerson hadn't been Terran's favourite person in the world, but at least Terran had never felt overly threatened by him. This new doctor, though…

The doctor hit a button on the intercom system and barked out an order for assistance. That damn trio of guards showed up seconds later. They had Terran strapped down tightly to the examination table before Terran could even put up a fight, then left as silently as they'd arrived.

The doctor hummed softly in contemplation, standing at the head of the table and studying Terran with cold eyes. Terran tilted his head back until he could study the hard features above him in return. The man was even uglier from upside down.

"I'm Dr Francis Crowton," the man announced.

"And that should mean something?" Terran snapped.

His little outburst was roundly ignored. "You are Terran Praetis."

"No shit."

"Stop being such a brat. Shall we discuss your little…biological peculiarities next, or shall I simply proceed with the tests?"

Terran didn't have a smart comeback this time, so he settled for a glare.

Crowton smiled. The sight wasn't pleasant. Terran swallowed the urge to start screaming right then and there.

Squeezing his eyes closed, Terran tried to burrow deep into his mind. The cold, sterile surroundings faded from his consciousness. But despite his best efforts, he wasn't able to close out the soft clink of metal and the acrid smell of antiseptic. Terran ground his teeth together and tried to stop the shudders that threatened to take over his body. He wasn't going to show the bastard how scared he was. *Am. Not.*

At the first prick of a needle, Terran wanted to scream for Daior. That damned so-called doctor was humming under his breath, a cheerful little tune, clearly enjoying his work. Terran was normally all for that attitude, except when said work involved Terran's pain and suffering.

Time blurred into an endless stream of pain and cold. Terran tried to fill his head with images, places, anything to distract him from the hell his reality had become. He clung to Daior's image with a fierce grip. Daior was okay and he was coming soon. Terran believed that with all his heart, he had to. Otherwise, he was going to turn into a screaming ball of…something. Hell, not even Terran's thoughts were making sense anymore. He couldn't focus. He kept trying to erect a wall around himself, keep reality out, but spikes of agony punched holes in his barrier nearly as fast as he could put it up.

Terran blinked bleary eyes open, staring blankly at the ceiling. He had no idea how much time had passed—minutes, hours, days, it all blurred together. Every square inch of his body ached and throbbed. A stream of blood trickled along his skin, running down his stomach and creating small puddles under his arms. Every breath sent shards of pain through his chest, like someone was ripping at the skin over and over. He was almost afraid to look and see the damage. Not that he could summon the energy to lift his head, anyway.

Metal clattered against metal as Crowton tossed something onto a nearby countertop. The noise almost drowned out the man's monotonous litany of curses.

"Damn splice," he spat. "Your body is as stubborn as your personality."

A small smile tried to work its way across Terran's face at that. All right, so maybe it wasn't much, but Terran was willing right now to get his kicks where he could. And the fact that Crowton was getting absolutely nowhere in his exploration? That was perversely satisfying.

"We'll try again tomorrow," the man declared. Long fingers stroked through Terran's hair roughly. "If the traditional methods won't work, we'll have to try more non-traditional tests. But I'd better get some sleep if I'm going to start pulling you apart piece by piece."

That killed Terran's slight amusement depressingly quickly. He held back a whimper as the door slid shut behind the doctor.

*Who knows?* Maybe Terran would get lucky and the bastard would die in his sleep. Terran figured the chances of that were pretty much non-existent, but the slender, illogical hope was really all he had right now.

"I need you, Dai," he whispered hoarsely to the empty room before letting his eyes slide closed and the darkness creep in.

* * * *

Tamesis Janssen had never expected to hear from Daior again. After all, the last words Daior had, well, yelled at him had been, "Come within a light year of me again and I'll rip your arms off."

Tam rather thought Daior had meant it at the time, too. So getting a distress call from his former partner had nearly been enough to send him into heart failure.

Tam leant back against the wall, tilting his chair on its rear legs. It hadn't taken him long to reach the outpost, which hovered on the edges of the more 'civilised' portions of the galaxy. He'd been cruising the trade routes already, a short jump away in his small cruiser. Less than a couple of hours in warp drive and presto, here he was, pretending to take a nap in an extremely uncomfortable wooden chair.

His current position on the small porch along the front of the tiny hostel provided an excellent view of the single, dusty street running from the pub at one end to the forest at the other. Tam propped his crossed ankles on the porch railing and tipped down his hat over his eyes. He was going for 'don't pay attention to me, just another miner'. Considering no one had looked twice at him in the last half hour, Tam figured he must be succeeding.

This was the part he was good at, the waiting. The observing.

Not that there was much to observe, really. The tiny town had more of the look of a mining encampment than any sort of permanent settlement. Several slapped together buildings fanned out around the pub, which seemed to serve as the town's central hub. Maybe a half-dozen buildings, tops, although there were lighter patches in the surrounding forest that might be houses or mines. Tam hadn't ventured into the thick gloom of the woods wrapped all around the town. His focus was elsewhere.

Namely, on the glint of metal that could be seen beyond the town limits. The small facility huddled up against the mountain, crouched about a half-mile from the end of the street. It was nearly hidden in the shadows of a copse of trees. The sheltering leaves, in an odd, creepy shade of grey, rustled softly in the occasional gust of wind.

This planet was far from inviting. Even as Tam kept an eye on the limited movement, he could hear the roars and squeals from the wilderness. Whatever was out there didn't sound friendly, that was for sure.

Trust Daior to get himself snared into a mess like this. It might have been ten years, but Tam's former partner had obviously changed very little. For the one with all the technological intelligence enhancements, Daior had an extremely bad tendency to leap first and think later. Tamesis, on the other hand, was the one who examined everything from every angle possible. Several times. Which was why he was lounging here, pretending to nap, instead of charging in brandishing weapons.

Tam often mused that the scientists who had put the pair of them together had got things arse-backwards. Served the idiots right for starting so early. The military group had performed the first enhancement surgeries when their orphaned subjects were only three years old. Amazing what a difference a few years would have made when it came to matching personalities with technology.

Tam's thoughts were jerked back to the present when a group of men walked past, laughing and joking. They were all in matching black uniforms, a strange, circle insignia patch on the shoulder. And they were all carrying weapons, some strapped to their hips, others slung over their backs.

One of the men shoved another playfully. The guard was sporting a large bandage on his cheekbone. The one he shoved had his finger in a splint and a white temp cast wrapped around his wrist.

*Bingo.*

Tam unobtrusively followed the group with his eyes, watching as they headed down the long, narrow trail from the facility in the distance. The uniformed men were the first clue Tam had found that the facility was guarded by more than just automated security systems. It was the final piece of information he needed.

Tam let his feet drop to the porch floor. He stood and stretched the kinks out of his back. Chairs were never big enough for his over-sized frame, and his hard, wooden perch had left him stiff and almost sore.

He nonchalantly descended the trio of steps onto the dusty street. Tam received a few suspicious looks as he strode past but no one approached him. This seemed like the type of place where people found it best to mind their own business. Just the kind of place Tam preferred.

It took him mere minutes to follow the small road past its curve and duck into the looming brush of the dense forest guarding the facility. He'd left his cruiser a half-mile away in a small clearing, and he headed back that way now. Time to load up on weapons, double-check his systems. Then it became a waiting game until dark.

Tam always worked better in the dark.

# Chapter Seven

Tamesis studied the prone bodies at his feet with narrowed eyes. Something about them tugged at his memory. Pale skin, curly dark hair, identical bulbous noses. He'd seen these men before, he would swear to it. Unless…

Tam shoved the thoughts to the back of his head. No time for puzzles right now. The Mystery of the Medical Facility Guards would have to wait until Tam finished his rescue mission. He hadn't failed at one of those yet and wasn't about to start now, when it really mattered.

Tam paused at the next intersection, nudging his scanning system into high gear. The building lay eerily quiet, but he was picking up a heat signature close by. Tam headed in that direction. If it were Terran or Dai, excellent. If not? He could have some more fun.

The second door Tam tried was locked. He smashed the sensor pad, shorting out the circuitry, and the door slid open. This room was dimly lit, and Tam smiled to himself with satisfaction.

A small sound drew his attention, and Tam gaped at the vision taking centre stage in the room. Pretty blue eyes blinked back tears before sliding closed. The boy turned his head away, seemingly resigned to whatever Tam had planned for him. Bright, carroty orange hair flopped over his face, and Tam's fingers itched. He wanted to bury them in the soft mass and trace the thin, blond streaks zigzagging through the strands.

Tam might not like it, might be jealous as anything, in fact, but you had to give Dai his due. The man had excellent taste.

The nylon restraints were fairly easy for Tam to rip apart, although judging by the red marks on Terran's wrists, they had certainly done their job.

"Are you okay, Terran?" he asked, removing the probe carefully before grabbing a towel and wiping some of the blood off the slender chest. Tam didn't want to move Terran until he was sure there wasn't any severe damage.

When silence answered his query, Tam gripped the young man's shoulder. It didn't escape his notice that his palm wrapped almost completely around it. "Hey," he called softly. "Hey. I'm Tamesis. It's okay. I'm here to help."

Terran accepted Tam's assistance in sitting up, but there was a mulish cast to his delicate features that shouted disbelief.

"Daior sent for me."

That announcement finally got Terran's attention, red head popping up, blue eyes narrowing.

Tam managed to summon up a small smile and held out his hand. He pushed up the cuff of his leather coat to show the small man his wrist.

"Oh." Terran reached out with slender, shaking fingers and stroked along the base of the tattoo curling around Tam's wrist and up his forearm. It was a perfect match to the one Daior sported. "You really know Dai?"

Tam nodded.

"Does he call you Tam?"

Tam was taken aback by the question, but he nodded again. Just like that, Terran relaxed, shoulders slumping in relief.

"Let's go find Dai, shall we?" Tam suggested. "Then we can all get out of here."

Terran hopped off the table, staggering when his bare feet hit the floor. Tam reached out to steady him, but the slender form was already in motion.

The room was wide and open, the narrow exam table the only piece of furniture. A row of counters ran along the walls, cabinets above them and wide, bin-like drawers beneath. Terran quickly dug through one of the bins until he produced some clothes and a pair of boots.

"I'm okay," he declared, finally answering Tam's question. "Just achy, mostly. It'll pass pretty quickly. Especially if…ah, there we go!"

Another search through one of the cabinets had produced a small vial. Tam stood back and let Terran go at it—he seemed to know precisely what he was doing. Terran expertly prepared the injection, his easy motions speaking of long practice. He slipped the needle into his hip, sighing a bare minute later, his whole body visibly relaxing.

"Ready," Terran announced. "Let's get the heck out of here."

The gentle hum of the air processor system was the only sound in the empty halls. Terran chewed on his lip, gaze darting left then right.

"Should I be concerned about guards?" Terran asked. "Because there weren't many of them, but they were really big and kind of mean and—"

"No," Tam interrupted shortly. He'd only found five on his trek through the facility, but none of them would be waking up soon. If at all. "Where to?" he asked. "Do you remember anything about where they stashed Dai?"

"It's that way." Terran pointed towards the left-hand corridor. "I think."

Tam followed the small man, keeping a close, concerned eye on the slight figure. Terran was weaving some, knees still unsteady. Whatever Terran had shot himself up with was helping, but the poor guy was still feeling the effects of his earlier ordeal. Tam really wished they could sit and let him recover some equilibrium, but there simply wasn't time. The guards were currently out of commission, but that still left a whole staff of other night time personnel, not to mention the security systems. And Tam hadn't been able to do as much recon as he normally liked. There could very well be an entire army lurking somewhere under the mountain, and he'd never know until far too late.

One shiny, eerily empty hallway blended into another until Terran brought their journey to a halt in front of an open door.

"No," Terran muttered. "No, this was it, I'm sure of it."

It might have been, but Daior was nowhere to be seen. Tam paced the confines of the small room, scanners working overtime for any little clue that might lead them to Dai.

"Do you think he's okay?" Terran asked.

Tam's head snapped up. Terran hovered in the doorway, panic written clearly on his face. Tam summoned up a reassuring smile, although judging by the way Terran's eyes narrowed, it wasn't a very effective one.

"He's alive," Tam assured him. And it was even the truth. They were still linked that much, anyway. Once upon a time, Tam would have been able to tell not only exactly where Dai was, but in what condition, down to the smallest bruise. Unfortunately, that wasn't the case anymore. He had to settle for the small, humming presence in the back of his head that signalled Daior was still in the land of the living.

While Tam scanned the inside of the room, Terran paced the narrow hall just outside. Terran's pert little nose stuck into the air, sniffing at regular intervals.

The little one suddenly stopped, eyes going wide.

"That way!" he declared, pointing back the way they'd come.

Tam had been around the universe a time or two. You learnt sometimes it was best not to question.

Besides, Terran was already halfway down the hall and nearly around the corner. Damn, the kid could move fast. But then again, so could Tam. His much longer legs enabled him to quickly outpace Terran as they raced through the maze of corridors. Blue steel nearly flashed by them, one wall blurring into another, each hallway looking far too much like the one before it. The facility wasn't that big inside, but it was built like a blasted corkscrew. It kept winding around until you weren't sure anymore which way was up. If not for Tam's tracking systems, they would most likely have been hopelessly lost in minutes.

Terran stopped outside a door right next to the medical bay where Tam had found him. Tam nearly snorted in self-disgust. They'd made a big circle and ended up right back where they'd started.

"This room, little one?" Tam asked. At Terran's nod, Tam slammed his shoulder against the flimsy door. It was cheap construction, old-fashioned hinges instead of a slide design, and popped open easily enough when he applied the right pressure.

Pitch darkness greeted him. Tam searched along the wall until he found a large pad. When he smacked it with his palm, flat rectangles of light began flickering to life. The room was long and narrow, shelving units stretching backwards, nearly groaning under the weight of neatly labelled boxes. Tam's gaze followed the trail of lighting as it illuminated the room until he spotted a crumpled figure nearly hidden behind an oversized metal crate.

Terran uttered a low cry, the sound full of distress and edged with panic, and pushed past Tam.

"Dai?" he called. "Oh, Gods. Dai?"

Terran dropped to his knees beside the prone figure. Blood splattered Dai's ripped clothing and left a dark trail across the floor.

"Let me look," Tam demanded. He breathed a sigh of relief when Dai's features came into view, a sigh that turned into a low expression of gratitude when he ran shaking hands over Dai's limp body.

"It's not his blood," Tam announced. "Or at least, not most of it."

Dai had been beaten, badly. But from Tam's brief assessment, he could tell there were no wounds big enough to cause the large amount of blood present. Dai must have found at least one of those guards Tam had missed. Probably several, from the look of him.

"I don't know if anything is broken, but we'll have to risk it," Tam continued.

"But—"

"He's not going to heal here, and I don't know how much longer we have until they realise you're both missing. I've got the equipment needed back on my ship."

Tam paused, watching the way Terran kept stroking Daior's hair. He softened a bit, some of his battle mode slipping.

"Hey," he called. Terran looked up. "He's tough."

As far as reassurances went, it wasn't the best, but Tam didn't have the time for anything more. He hoisted Daior into his arms with a low grunt. Man weighed a bloody ton.

Terran fluttered around them like a jacked-up rabbit. "Is he going to be okay? Tamesis? He's still breathing, right?"

"Yes and yes," Tam said. "Now move."

Tam kept their pace swift as they worked their way back through the complex, Terran trailing him like a little shadow, silent and surefooted. An audible exclamation of relief burst from the small man when the double-wide compressor doors came into view, their key to the outside world.

Tam wouldn't let himself relax until they were on his ship and several light-years away. His cynicism was rewarded when an extremely obnoxious alarm blared its warning. Terran squealed, jumping about a foot and clapping his hands over his ears.

"Move!" Tam bellowed, shoving the little one in front of him while juggling Dai's dead weight in his arms. "Go, now!"

Terran went. They ran for the door, panic heavy enough in the air to almost taste. Terran smacked the release pad, and they slipped through mere seconds before the emergency systems kicked in. The doors slammed back together behind them, sealing closed with a small, warning buzz.

"Straight ahead," Tam ordered. "Through that yellow bush."

They crashed through the forest that sheltered the facility. The blue-grey walls faded behind them, the thick brush swallowing them quickly. Tam led them unerringly across the small trails made by animals, taking a path parallel to the facility. On their left the land rose, large boulders resting against the trunks of trees as the landscape gave way from rolling foothills to craggy mountains. It was a heart-pounding five minutes before a glint of moonlight on metal shone ahead of them. Tam pushed between a small stand of green, prickly trees and out into a narrow meadow. His cruiser waited, barely fitting in the small, open space. Thank the stars for vertical thrusters. Clear land was at a premium around here.

It took only seconds for Tam to hit the unlocking sequence, open the door and lower the short docking ramp. The interior lights of the *Farion* flickered on the instant his boot hit the floor inside.

"I have to get Dai settled," Tam stated. "Don't suppose you know how to fly one of these things?"

Terran snorted. "Are you kidding? I've been flying since I could walk."

Tam wasn't surprised. Most kids learnt to fly these days. And with that lithe build and his quick reflexes? Terran was probably one hell of a pilot.

"Then get to it," Tam ordered. "I've got the system set for a fast start. Just get the engines up and running. I'll be there in a few minutes to take over. Then we can get the hell off this rock."

They parted ways, Tam's steps rapid. He looked down at the still face, so familiar. A few more lines, face bones a bit more prominent albeit nearly hidden by that bushy mass masquerading as a beard. But still the same man. Still his Daior. Worry niggled at the edges of his mind, but Tam firmly ignored it. He had work to do.

After they made their escape would be soon enough to worry about Daior. And about what came next. For all three of them.

Terran darted to the bridge and slid into the chair in front of the main console. He was slapping buttons before the chair finished swivelling forward. He flicked the big, red switch for the core engines and a satisfying rumble sent vibrations through the floor. Terran grinned widely. *Oh, yeah. Listen to that baby purr.* This? This was one sweet ship.

"Hang on," he sang into the intercom. "This might be a bit rough."

Terran didn't bother with the flight support features. Those were for amateurs. And Terran was anything but an amateur in the cockpit. If it moved through space, he could fly it. Extremely well.

He wrapped his hands around the yoke, tilted the whole thing back to edge up the nose of the ship then engaged the thrusters. The ship bucked a bit, resisting what he wanted, before rising to hover a few feet above the ground. Terran stared hard at the instruments, waiting for the engine revolutions to reach just the right speed.

The radio hummed into life. "Virgo One Starship, you are in a restricted zone. Disengage engines and identify yourself."

Terran snorted derisively and smacked off the squawking instrument. As if he were going to answer the bastards.

The needle of the RPM gauge inched into the red just as Tam dropped into the co-pilot's seat. Terran yanked back on the wheel and the little ship jumped vertically into the air.

"Did you get Dai settled okay?" Terran asked anxiously, hands moving automatically through the familiar motions. "Is he okay?"

Tam gripped the arm of his chair with white knuckles. "Holy Christ, boy, watch what you're doing!"

"I am."

"Trees! Trees!"

"I'm not going to hit the trees," Terran declared in disgust. He skimmed the tops of the odd, grey foliage with a satisfying brush and only minimal scraping. His plan was to stay low until he could get the engine's revolutions up a bit more, high enough to make a dash straight up. He wanted through the gravitational field without any bog-down. Tam would just have to stay anxious until they hit outer space.

"Holy—I thought you said you could fly!"

"I can. Stop being such a baby."

"A bab—Mountain!"

"For the love of the Gods, will you shut up?" Terran snapped.

The whine of the engines increased as Terran pushed the little starship to her limits. *Ah, there it is.*

"Wooohooo!" Terran whooped. He slammed on the thrusters and the cruiser shot into a vertical climb. The force threw them back in their seats, the ship slowing only slightly as they cleared the clouds and the atmospheric pull dragged against the hull.

When they emerged on the other side of the planet's atmosphere, it was like launching out of a slingshot. The ship barrelled through space at impressive speed. Terran dodged a couple of meteors with ease before giving the engines a much-needed break. He switched on the warp drive and leant back, stretching, utterly satisfied with his performance.

"She's fantastic," Terran told Tam, patting the console affectionately. "Handles like a dream. We'll just hang here in warp until you let me know where you want to go."

"I ought to put you over my knee," came the hoarse reply.

Terran laughed aloud at the ferocious glare coming his way. "What, you don't like the way I fly?"

"You really don't want to go there right now. I think my stomach is still planet-side."

Despite his snide tone, one corner of Tam's mouth kicked up a bit.

"Where do I point her?" Terran asked, sobering abruptly as a picture of a bloodied and battered Daior popped into his head. "Does Dai... Does Dai need a medical unit?"

Tam stood, doing a bit of stretching of his own. He tossed his long, leather jacket over the chair and shook his head. "No, a medical unit wouldn't be able to help him."

The blood drained from Terran's face as horror ripped through him.

"They just wouldn't know how to deal with Dai's physiology," Tam hastened to reassure Terran, looking a bit panicked himself for a brief instant. "I've got a pretty well-equipped medical bay of my own, all the equipment I need to handle an Advanced Tek. I'm running a diagnostic, but it'll take about an hour. I'll know more then, although I didn't see anything too serious. Looks like he might have a broken leg, a couple of cracked ribs and a magnificent collection of bruises and scrapes, nothing life-threatening. Nothing my EHU can't handle."

Terran sighed in genuine relief. An EHU, or Extraneous Healing Unit, could piece together most general injuries. They were insanely expensive, though. It surprised Terran that Tam actually had one. Not that he was complaining.

Tam squeezed Terran's shoulder. "He isn't going to leave you."

Terran nodded, not even able to get words of thanks out around the lump in his throat. He reached up, put his hand over Tam's and squeezed back.

Tam nodded gruffly, message received and acknowledged. "I'm going to go get cleaned up."

Terran turned his chair on its pivot, watching Tam leave. Now that the pressure was off, that they were free and clear of that damned planet, exhaustion rolled over him. He wasn't too tired, though, to scrutinize the way substantial muscles bunched under the fabric of Tam's black T-shirt. The long, silky blond braid swayed gently, ends brushing against the top of a truly mouth-watering arse. Terran really wanted to tag after Tam, ask him some questions, but he couldn't summon the energy.

This man, though, had been important to Daior. Really important. Important enough that Daior had called Tam's name in his sleep.

Terran double-checked the ship's settings through barely open eyes before sliding down farther into the extremely large and comfortable pilot's chair. Not standard ship issue, these. Forget finding a bed. Terran thought he might just fall asleep right here.

And later, he and Tam were going to have a nice, long talk.

# Chapter Eight

Terran glared, scowling with all the ferocity he could muster at Tam's retreating arse. Admittedly, it was a very nice view. Terran would just prefer it wasn't the only part of Tam he saw lately.

Tam disappeared around the corner, mumbling something about electrical shorts in the reactor. The *Farion* didn't have a reactor—no ship nowadays did—but Terran let him go anyway. No point in following. Tam must think Terran had some kind of highly communicable disease. Whenever Terran walked into a room, Tam walked out.

Terran headed in the opposite direction, down the gleaming corridor and up a nearby staircase. The metal steps curved up one wall, and he followed them to his favourite hiding place.

The second level of the *Farion* was much smaller than the first, really a big room that formed a bubble on the top of the predominately sleek-lined vessel. The large, open area formed a gathering place scattered with couches and fluffy chairs. Most of the floor up here was covered in a thick carpet that invited a person to sprawl in front of the large entertainment console. Narrow windows, spaced evenly around the circular walls, provided small alcoves at various intervals. The entire ceiling was arched, a high-tempered glass skylight to the depths of space around them.

Terran plopped onto one of the window seats with a sigh. He bunched up a pair of pillows and shoved them behind his back, hugged his knees to his chest and watched the still view outside his chosen window.

He hated space. Hated, *hated.* It was vast and boring and claustrophobic. Oh, he supposed the thousands of glittering lights and the occasional bursts of colour were pretty enough in their own way. But to Terran, it all seemed so empty. So lifeless.

He leaned his forehead against the cold window, curling tighter into himself in a vain attempt to soothe the cramp in his stomach. It always started this way. A gnawing, constant ache that no amount of painkillers could eliminate. Unfortunately, it was only the first step on a short stairway that led to…unpleasant things.

Terran really wanted to talk to Daior first and explain everything. But Dai still lay in the medical ward, sleeping deeply. According to Tam, it would be a few more days before Dai woke up. Something about reconstruction. Tam's explanation had made little sense to Terran. Not that mechanics and technology were Terran's strong point, but then again, Tam's lecture had been a bit short on details.

"What are you doing up here?" Tam asked.

Terran shrugged, turning his attention back to the dull vista outside his window. "Just thinking. I got tired of watching Dai sleep, and you didn't seem to be in the mood for conversation."

"Maybe I am now." Tam strode across the room to stand by Terran's shoulder. "You don't need to worry, you know. Dai will be just fine."

Terran would have appreciated the assurance if it had come in a less patronising tone. His surge of anger, though, caught him by surprise. It was a bit of an extreme reaction to what should have been nothing more than a minor annoyance.

*Damn biology.* It looked like he was going to be forced to have that talk with Tam, after all. Dai could be out for days yet. Terran didn't think he was going to be able to wait that long.

"How far to the safest port?" Terran asked.

"I'd have to check," Tam admitted. "Quite frankly, I'm not entirely sure where we are. This part of the universe is beyond my normal range."

Terran snorted, anger melting into amusement, although there was a dark edge to the emotion. "Really? With as often as you've been staring at the instruments, I thought you'd be able to quote our exact position. Down to the centimetre."

Tam's cheeks flushed a dull red. It was an odd look on the harsh features. Not to mention turning Tam's pale skin blotchy. The man really didn't blush well. "I haven't been paying that much attention to what I'm looking at," he said.

"Do tell."

"Enough with the attitude," Tam snapped. "I'm on your side here. A little politeness wouldn't go amiss."

"Sorry." Terran meant the apology. He knew he could be a real brat sometimes. He tried, but there wasn't always much he could do to prevent the attitude issues. "I'm just…itchy."

Tam heaved a sigh of his own as he sat down next to Terran. He crossed his legs on the long, cushioned bench, turning so he faced Terran. "Want to talk about it?"

"Not really, but I think I have to."

"Does this have anything to do with why those scientists were so eager to get their hands on you?"

"Maybe."

"Care to elaborate?"

"Not really," Terran said again.

"Try anyway."

Terran huffed out his annoyance. Tam crossed his arms and stared.

Terran was a master at the stubbornness game, but today Tam's piercing stare was getting right through Terran's normally impervious shell. Terran looked away. He grabbed one of the brightly coloured, squishy pillows wedged between him and the window and hugged it close. When Terran realised he was making senseless patterns on the fabric with his fingers, he forced himself to stop.

"I'm a bother, aren't I?" he muttered.

"Say what?"

Terran started chewing on his lower lip. "A bother. Burden. Trouble magnet. My brother has about a dozen more similar nicknames for me. Pick one."

"What the hell does that have to do with your current predicament?" Tam asked, voice vibrating with confusion.

"Everything," Terran groused.

"Terran."

"I don't want to do this right now." And damn, but could he sound more like a whiny three year old? He didn't think so.

"Terran."

A harsh edge had crept in past Tam's confusion, and just like that, Terran caved. Fuck, he had the spine of a jellyfish today.

"No one's talking back home," Terran stated. He waved away Tam's sour look, which was a clear demand for clarification. "Just wait, I'm getting there. No one knows what happened, or how, or why. Well, obviously someone knows, probably my dad, 'cause he knows everything. But he isn't saying a word and—"

"Terran!"

"Sorry, sorry!" Terran took a deep breath and forced his mind back on track. No more rambling. Tam was clearly losing patience. Terran didn't blame him, either. "My point is, I was always a weird kid, kind of hyper and spastic. But when I turned thirteen, my world went to hell in a hand basket. Boom, overnight my hair went strange coloured and I got these insane mood swings. My mouth itched for a solid week and, well, when it was over I had these." Terran opened his mouth and pointed, displaying his small, extremely pointy fangs.

"All right, unusual, sure, but not unhear—"

"I'm a splice."

"Come again?" Tam asked.

"Splice," Terran enunciated. "You know, mostly human with a little animal DNA mixed in for laughs?"

Tam shook his head slowly, pale brows furrowing. "Splicing is illegal."

"Yeah, tell me about it."

"All right, about three or four decades—"

"Sarcasm, man," Terran interrupted again. "I know the story."

Everyone knew the story. The fad had ripped through several solar systems decades ago, one more attempt by man to make a 'better' human. At first it had been just screwing around with various humanoid DNA. No biggie, as everyone's base DNA could be traced back to Earth at some point or another.

Then scientists had started trying to artificially cross-breed several not-quite-as-humanoid species. The ones biologically incompatible with humans, despite their shared ancestry. The ones who had evolved so completely in their new environments that they ended up with things like extra limbs and weird body shapes. The results of the experiment had been...interesting, to say the least.

When those same scientists had started mixing human and animal genetics together, the Naturide Federation had stepped in and said 'enough is enough'. Lines had to be drawn and, as with cloning, the Federation eventually banned the entire process.

"You're too young to have been a by-product of the splicing craze," Tam pointed out logically. "Besides that, most of those particular experiments had pretty short life-spans. The genetic structure was far too unstable."

Terran could see it in his eyes—Tam didn't want Terran's words to be true. Tam clearly realised how complicated the situation would become if he had an actual splice on his hands.

Unfortunately, Terran couldn't change reality. If he could, he would have done it ages ago, gone home to

Altaireon and lived quite happily out from under the all-too-watchful eye of Richard.

"A splice," Tam muttered. He rubbed one hand over his neatly-trimmed beard, lips pursing in their blond frame. "Holy hell. And no one has any idea how it happened?"

Terran shrugged and started playing with his pillow again. "Like I said, no one's talking. I guess I understand. It's not like they can do anything about it. It would just be nice, you know? Understanding where the heck my freakish self came from?"

"Don't call yourself a freak," Tam snapped. "You're different. So what? I met a guy from Venus once. You want to see weird? That was one planet that never should have been colonised."

"If it was just the looks and the damn purring, I could handle it!" Terran burst out. He tossed the pillow away, watching it slide across the slick floor until it hit the edge of the giant, red rug in the middle of the room. "But it's not. I get antsy and distractible, bounce from one activity to another so fast I get whiplash. I'm like a kid with ADHD on crack. And don't even get me started on the mood swings. One minute I'm hanging from the ceiling and ten seconds later I'm bawling my eyes out. It's awful. I'm usually on medication to control the worst of the by-products."

"Terran—"

Terran stuffed his fist in his mouth, muffling a sob. "Too long and I get sick. My DNA is pretty much tacked together with wire and glue. I've already gone through the nausea and headache phase and we're into the twitchy skin and aching stomach phase. Pretty soon I won't be able to keep any solid food down at all, and my skin will get super sensitive and then comes the pain and—"

"What do you need?"

That simple question, stated so evenly, calmed Terran like nothing else could have. He looked up and met Tam's eyes with desperate hope.

"You're not mad?" he asked.

"Mad?" Tam's face was going to be permanently stuck in confusion pretty soon. "Why the hell would I be mad? Like you said, it's not like you can do anything to change your genetics."

"You're really not upset," Terran stated with wonder. He rose up on his knees, bracing his hands on Tam's thick biceps, moving in close to stare intently into Tam's ice blue eyes.

Tam's firm lips tipped up into a smile as he stared back. "Terran, in case you haven't noticed, I'm not exactly normal myself. I don't know how much Daior told you, but we were part of an experiment ourselves. I'm different, you're different. It is what it is, and I don't see any reason to get upset."

Terran sat back, gnawing on his lower lip. Tam reached out and gently freed the soft flesh, rubbing his thumb over the cracked and abused skin.

"You'll hurt yourself," Tam chided softly.

Terran smiled, feeling an equal mix of shyness and relief. "You really don't think I'm an abomination," he stated, seeing the truth in Tam's eyes.

His remark earned a dark scowl and a vicious curse from Tam. "Who the fuck called you an abomination?"

Terran looked away again and shrugged.

"Hey." Tam grabbed Terran's chin firmly and forced eye contact again. "There is nothing wrong with you," he said emphatically. "You didn't ask to be different. Anyone who blames you for something you had no control over is an idiot and doesn't deserve a single second of your time."

*Oh.* Terran's heart just melted, right then and there, opening up and creating a Tam-sized place right next to Daior. Terran reached out and wrapped his hand around Tam's wrist, halting the big man when Tam would have moved away. Then Terran turned his head, placed a brief kiss against the soft skin of Tam's palm and nuzzled happily.

A look of dismay crossed Tam's features just before he snatched his hand back. He stood swiftly, that blasted remote expression dropping over his face again. Terran wanted to pout. He liked Tam's touch, liked feeling those big hands on his skin, so strong yet so gentle. But every time he tried to get close, Tam ran the other way. Darn the man and his overly developed sense of propriety.

"You never told me what you needed," Tam stated quickly.

Terran decided to let the issue go. This time.

"Medicine," he stated. "A place where I can get my hands on some unusual drugs. Then a spot to work up a compound, either by finding a chemist or the equipment to do it myself."

"All right." Tam nodded decisively. "That I can do. Come on, Little Bit. Let's go take a look at the map and get you what you need."

Tam was halfway down the stairs before Terran even stood. Terran watched that magnificent arse disappear from view once again and manfully shoved down the desire that had him half-hard and wanting.

Desire, no matter how strong, would have to wait. There were more pressing issues to deal with.

At the top of that list was retribution for that really awful nickname. Terran was short, he knew it, accepted it. Didn't mean he wanted to be reminded of it. And he was just going to have to kick Tam's seven foot bum to prove it.

# Chapter Nine

The Indara Space Station, massive and humming with life, loomed on the edges of the Myrian Galaxy. Of all the Stations scattered around the many known worlds, it was by far the largest. The shopping district alone sprawled for several kilometres. And it only took up a fraction of one of the Station's six decks.

As they stepped out of the lift, Tam inhaled deeply, welcoming the familiar scent of spices that overwhelmed the normal smells of ionised air and grease. He loved this place, full of music and colour. While roaming the Indara Bazaar, it was easy to forget about being completely enclosed in a metal hull. Reds and oranges dominated and exotic and hypnotic music rose above the chattering voices, the influences of the nearest solar system. Tam had read once that this area had been heavily settled by immigrants from Earth's Eastern cultures, and it showed.

The Eastern cultures were popular on the Stations. The hulking structures were usually the last bastions of civilisation, placed along the main shipping routes where no usable planets were available. For Tam, the bright colours and rich smells always came as a huge relief after living for months in the cold black of space. He figured most people, human or not, shared his view.

"This way," Tam directed, taking Terran's arm and guiding him around a group of brightly decorated people.

"Oh, wait." Terran tried to pull away to get a closer look at the courtesans.

Tam yanked him back. "Horny brat."

"And proud of it. Did you see the skinny guy? I think his whole body was one giant tattoo. It was really hot."

Tam sighed. "Focus, brat." Traitorous mind, wondering what Terran would think of Tam's own tats. *Bad Tam. Bad.*

They had a mission. An important one. A complicated one, too. Figure out what Terran needed. Keep the three of them under the radar. Make sure those bastards chasing them didn't get their hands on Tam's guys again. Because they would definitely try. *Okay, sure. No problem.*

Who was he kidding? This was a nightmare. But Tam wasn't about to back out now. *No way, no how.* Even if he had a choice, which he rather suspected he didn't. If they knew about Daior, then they knew about him.

First things first. Get Terran back on his meds. Preferably before the kid shot into orbit. Even now, Terran was bouncing—skipping, actually—alongside Tam. Although some of the skipping might have less to do with hyperactive excitement and more to do with Terran's short legs. Tam noted with amusement that one of his own strides was about equal to three of Terran's.

"Where are we going?" Terran asked, head swinging from side to side as he tried to see everything at once.

"There's a clinic a few halls down. They should have what you need."

Terran followed Tam through the twisted, haphazard alleys of vendors. "You know your way around here really well," he observed. "It's impressive."

"Indara is something of my home base," Tam said. "I spend a lot of time here."

"Your home base? Do you have a…what do they call it? A berth?"

Tam laughed. "Wrong type of vessel, Bit. But yes, I do have a place here." It was tiny, one of many boltholes scattered among various planets and Stations. After all, a mercenary had to be prepared.

"Cool. Will I get to see it?"

Tam dragged Terran away from a display of meat pies. "Damn. You remind me of a puppy. No attention span at all."

"I can focus," Terran protested. "And I resent that. There's nothing remotely canine about me."

Tam rolled his eyes and kept a firm grasp on Terran's wrist. What he really needed was one of those little leash things you sometimes saw mothers and small kids with. Tie Terran to him. Otherwise, he just might lose the little man in the throng.

"Oh!"

Terran yanked Tam to a halt, staring with wide, blue eyes at a brilliantly plumed parrot. Tam didn't like the look in Terran's eyes, not one bit. They *really* needed to get their hands on that medication. Humans didn't normally look that hungry when they examined live birds.

"Terran!"

"So pretty."

"Focus, Terran. You can't eat the pretty bird."

Terran shook himself, wrinkling his nose. "It's probably all feathers, anyway."

"Right."

They began moving again through the busy market, Tam forging the way through the crowd. Terran, in a sudden burst of uncertainty, clung tightly to Tam's hand. Tam savoured the feel of the fingers wrapped so trustingly around his own. The small man was such an interesting mix of shy and reckless, innocent and headstrong. Tam tried fiercely, again, to clamp down on his growing fascination. This one was off limits. Daior would flay him alive, and Tam wouldn't blame him one bit for it, either.

They'd made good progress through the throng and to their goal when it was Tam's turn to stop abruptly. He swung in a slow circle, eyes scanning the nearby crowd. He could have sworn…

Terran tugged on his hand. "Tam?" he asked, voice low and worried. "Did you see something?"

"Maybe."

*Initiate scan.*

"Keep moving."

*No imminent threat detected.*

At the report from his computer systems, Tam relaxed, but only slightly. His systems, after all, had been known to be wrong. His mental enhancements and augmentations weren't quite as developed as

Daior's. Technologically speaking, Tam was the brawn of the pair.

Tam kept a close eye on Terran, breathing a sigh of relief when they finally left the main bazaar behind. The huge, open space was ostensibly reserved for temporary vendors, although most of those were temporary in name only. They shifted their stalls a few feet every couple of weeks to keep their licenses. Some, however, travelled back and forth between the different ports, both land-bound and floating. The bazaar was, however, where the majority of the trading was done.

On the far side of it, they entered the private sectors of the Station. Here, a stately indoor mall stretched for several corridors, nearly a quarter of a mile long. It was where the permanent residents did their shopping. It was also, to put it bluntly, the domain of the wealthy. The people here were just as colourful as the people in the bazaar, but the fabrics they wore were richly patterned silks, and they had servants striding in their wake. The displays in the shop windows they passed boasted wares with prices that made Tam want to cringe.

Needless to say, they weren't here to shop. He turned at a corner billboard decorated with signs, an almost equal mix of advertisements and business names. There, just ahead, was their goal. A pair of double glass doors stood propped open underneath a brightly lit sign declaring 'Indara Medical Complex'.

Indara Med was famous in this region. The outer area combined a pharmacy and clinic, the latter of which boasted some of the most skilled physicians in the area. It was the back room, however, that generated the most business and accounted primarily for the complex's fame. Whatever drugs Indara Med didn't have, they could get. Legal or illegal, the source didn't matter. Tam wasn't ashamed to admit he had conducted a few of his own less than legal transactions here. From both ends.

Inside the brightly lit interior, a perky nurse with fluffy hair and a painted-on smile greeted them. "Here for an exam?" she asked cheerfully.

"No," Tam said shortly, pushing past her with barely a glance. "And for the Gods' sakes, Mercy, stop acting like you don't know me. It hasn't been that long."

"Shove it out the cargo bay, Tamesis," came the tart reply.

Tam shook his head, still dragging Terran, as he made quick progress across the waiting room and into the pharmacy. A few people looked up from their work to wave as they went past, but no one tried to stop them as they wove through the rows of counters. Tam gave a brief nod to the technician who opened the secured door in the back for them, and went right in.

"They know you pretty well here," Terran remarked.

Tam just grunted. Now really wasn't the best time to go into detail regarding his less-than-pristine career.

They found Dr. Marvin Mercuride—and no one would ever be able to convince Tam that was the bastard's real name—right where he usually was. The chemist hid in a little nook, surrounded by towering metal shelves full of bottles and containers. He tapped away at a keyboard, muttering to himself. Probably in multiple languages. Glasses perched on the end of his narrow nose, and his unruly brown hair, in desperate need of a cut, stood on end. No lab coat for the good doctor. His jeans sported a nice collection of holes, and his T-shirt bore some weird slogan, faded so badly the words were no longer identifiable. That was okay. It was probably offensive.

Hell, Tam was just grateful the bastard was wearing clothes at all. On one memorable occasion, Tam had walked in to find Marv dressed in a pair of polka-dotted boxers. Pink ones. Tam had been plagued with nightmares for weeks after that little incident.

"Marvin!" Tam yelled.

Marvin and Terran both jumped. Marv swirled on his stool, glaring at them both over the top of his glasses.

"Gods, do you have to do that?"

"Only if I want to get your attention."

Marv sighed. "All right, what do I have to do this time to get you to go away?"

"I need some supplies. Meds. Unusual ones."

A look crept into Marvin's eyes, one that Tam could only label fanatical. He half-expected Marv to rub his hands together and start cackling. The man did love a good medical mystery. In fact, he was damn near obsessive about it.

"Oh? Maybe I can help. You know, medication isn't always—"

"Just get us the stuff," Tam interrupted "I didn't come here to play doctor with you."

Terran poked Tam in the back. Tam grunted at the force but otherwise ignored him. Tam wasn't introducing the little fugitive to any more people than necessary. And while he considered Marvin a friend, that didn't mean the chemist could be trusted.

"Pity." Marv stood and stretched, shirt riding up to expose a surprisingly fit abdomen. For all his quirks and general weirdness, Marv was actually a pretty good looking guy. He just had very little interest in people, male or female. If it didn't come in Latin or involve a mutating virus, the good doctor simply didn't care.

Marvin seemed to notice Terran for the first time. One shaggy eyebrow rose, something about the smaller man apparently catching Marvin's interest. That was the last thing Tam wanted, but they really had no choice. Marv was the only one in this part of the universe capable of helping them.

"Who is this, Tam?" Marvin asked, peering intently.

"A friend," Tam replied vaguely. Terran had stopped poking Tam and was now trying to hide behind his back. The earlier bounce seemed to have worn off into a sudden bout of very un-Terran-like shyness. "Tell the doctor what you need, Terran."

"Trouble, Tam?" Marvin asked.

"Always," Tam replied.

Terran began to rattle off a series of long, chemical names. Tam couldn't follow most of it, but Marv didn't have any problems. Despite the warehouse setting, all the requested medications were gathered and deposited on a low table within minutes.

"There you are," Marvin announced. "Payment method as usual."

"There's more."

"Of course there is."

"It's tricky," Tam mused, rubbing at his chin. Mostly to hide the grin. "I'm not sure if you can pull it off."

Marvin straightened his shoulders, glaring. "Just what can't I do?"

"Well, we need all that," Tam said, waving a hand at the rather impressive collection of bottles and containers, "mixed into one handy-to-administer concoction."

Marvin's dark eyes widened, and he cursed. "Please tell me you're joking."

"Hardly. Bit, can you—"

Tam turned around only to discover that sometime in the last thirty seconds, Terran had vanished. *Hellfire and brimstone.*

"Did you see where he went?" Tam demanded.

It was Tam's turn to curse when Marv shook his head.

"Damn it, if he went back for that damn parrot..."

"Should I even ask?"

"No. Just see what you can do with all that crap while I track him down."

"You know, I'd love to, Tam. I really would. And while I may be the most brilliant mind on all of Indara, even I need more to go on than 'combine it'."

"I've got someone with unstable DNA. You need to stabilise it."

"Alien or human?"

"Both. I think."

"You're determined to make this difficult, aren't you?"

"Marv, I don't have time." Tam had himself halfway out of the door and kept inching farther every second. He didn't have time to play twenty questions. He needed to find Terran. Now. "Just do what you can."

"Tam!"

*Shit.* There was no help for it. "Splice," he spat. "You're fixing a splice. Now get to it."

He turned and ran from the room, Marv's sputtering shouts following him.

# Chapter Ten

No one paid Tam any attention as he hit the street, heading back towards the bazaar. Many of the stores near the clinic were closing down for the evening, leaving empty hallways, but no small, orange-haired troublemaker was in sight.

Tam growled under his breath and closed his eyes long enough to initiate a scan. Unfortunately, he hadn't taken the time to put any kind of tracking chip in Terran yet. That was the first thing he was going to do when they got back to the *Farion*, that was for sure. For now, he'd have to rely on body type recognition and manually sort through the candidates.

Damn, but he wished Dai were here. Tam's tracking systems were almost elementary in comparison to those of his former partner. A search that would take Daior five minutes would take Tam nearly three times as long, at the least.

Tam quickly trekked back through the rapidly emptying mall and to the market district. The more upscale shops might have been closing down, but the bazaar was busier than ever. The number of courtesans weaving through the masses had nearly doubled, the nightlife of the Station coming out to play.

"Damn it, Terran," Tam growled, glaring around the crowded marketplace. He moved a few feet to the left, peering over heads but still not seeing the one bright one he sought. All his focus went towards finding Terran, and he paid little attention to where he was going, muttering random apologies as he bumped into people and trampled on feet. One collision sent his victim staggering and Tam absently righted the person.

He jerked, looking down, when said person pressed close.

A woman wearing thick eyeliner, a couple of strategically placed handkerchiefs and not much else smiled up at him, running a hand down his arm. "Something I can help you with, big boy?" she purred.

Tam nearly rolled his eyes but settled for shrugging her off. "Sorry," he replied shortly. "I'm looking for someone, and you're not him."

He pushed past the pouting girl and kept moving, circling the edges of the crowd, wading through the results his scanning programme sent him at a headache-inducing pace. Who knew there were so many small, wiry men running around Indara?

*There.* The tiny person in quadrant four looked promising.

Tam shoved through the sea of bodies, using his bulk to plough a path. Most people took one look at him—mainly his size, although the fierce expression probably didn't hurt—and bit back any complaints.

The crowd ended abruptly and Tam nearly fell into the shadows behind the merchant stalls.

"Now where…?" he muttered.

"Tam!"

Tam whirled around, scowling and cursing. Behind him? How the heck did Terran get behind him? Tam left the shadows again, rounding the corners of several stalls and emerging back into the crowd. *Damn it to the Seventh Ring.* He knew Terran was here. Somewhere. He'd just heard him. It was like playing hide and seek. And Tam had always hated that game with a passion.

An explosion of shouts and curses erupting to the left stopped Tam in his tracks. He quickly changed course.

"Five to one I know who caused *that,*" he snarled. A passing man, dark and swarthy, gave Tam a glare. Tam glared back, mentally making a note to work on that whole talking-out-loud habit he'd fallen into. *Too much time alone.*

Tam wasn't the slightest bit surprised to find Terran smack dab in the middle of the disturbance. Resigned, maybe, but not surprised. Tam's small charge stood toe-to-toe with a large, burly idiot. The man was nearly as tall as Tam, arms thick and muscled, and had the look of a sailor off one of the massive barges that brought supplies to the outer Stations and planets. Overall, not the kind of person you generally wanted to mess with.

That didn't seem to bother Terran at all. Nor did the fact that the sailor had at least eight inches of height over Terran, not to mention a good hundred and fifty pounds. Terran practically bounced in his boots, bright hair puffier than usual. Fierce eyes glared up, the blue almost swallowed by his pupils. Terran actually hissed at the sailor in anger, the expression revealing two tiny, pointed teeth.

Tam stopped a ways from them, crossed his arms and tried not to laugh. Really, he shouldn't find the scene amusing. And he sure as hell shouldn't think Terran looked cute, all riled up like that. He couldn't help it.

The amusement vanished, however, when the sailor took a swing at Tam's little cat. Terran ducked easily, making a noise reminiscent of an angry yowl.

Tam covered the distance between them, just in time to catch the sailor's upraised fist.

"I wouldn't do that if I were you," Tam warned with a vicious glare.

"Stay out of this," the sailor snapped.

"Sorry, can't do that."

The man tried to pull his hand away, and Tam tightened his grip, jerking on the arm he held. "Try to hit him again and I'll rip your arm off."

"He'd do it, too," Terran said. He poked his head around Tam, smirking at the sailor from under Tam's upraised arm.

Tam tossed the man's hand away, barely noticing the way the big man rubbed at his wrist, and turned his glare on Terran. "What part of 'stay close' did you not understand?" he demanded.

At least Terran had the good sense to look ashamed. "I was hungry," he defended.

Tam didn't know whether to laugh or scream. He settled for rubbing his forehead, a vain attempt to soothe the growing pounding. "You went back for the bird, didn't you?"

Terran shrugged.

"The bird was nearly a block back," Tam pointed out.

Terran pointed at his adversary, nearly stabbing the man in the chest with his finger. "I was on my way to find you," he insisted, "but *he* tripped me."

"The little runt attacked me!" The man blustered. "Came at me for no reason and kicked me in the shin!"

"How the heck did you even feel it?" Tam asked wryly, looking down at the man's thickly muscled legs.

"Hey!"

Tam ignored Terran's indignation. "Terran is sorry," he said. "He offers his deepest apologies."

"No, I don't!"

"Yes, you do," Tam snapped, dragging Terran away. Once more, blustery protests followed, but Tam ignored the bewildered crowd to scold Terran. "What the hell was that about?"

"I don't know."

*Oh, damn.* Tam sighed. He shifted his grip from tugging to holding hands when Terran's lower lip started quivering. Then tears welled up in the once again blue eyes, and Tam's stomach knotted with tension.

"Don't do that," he ordered, feeling a slight surge of panic. "Damn, I see what you meant about the mood swings."

Terran wailed and leapt into Tam's arms. Tam staggered, barely keeping them upright, and patted Terran awkwardly on the back.

"It's okay," he said, trying frantically to soothe the suddenly hysterical man. "Marv's mixing up a magic potion for you as we speak. You'll feel better soon."

Terran sniffed but didn't fight when Tam untangled them. The small man wiped his nose on his sleeve, blinking the tears away. "Okay," he said. He took a couple of deep breaths, visibly calming down.

"There. Feel better, Little Bit?"

Wrong thing to say. Terran's face flushed and his eyes narrowed, black once again swallowing the blue.

"Don't call me that," he growled. "I'm not little."

Considering that Terran was all of five foot six, over a foot shorter than Tam, well, that made him pretty damn little.

"I meant it as a compliment," Tam explained. "You're little and cute and—"

"You think I'm cute?"

*Dang.* Tam practically needed a psychic to keep up with the mental leaps of the squirt's agile brain. Tam sighed and rubbed his head again. That headache was growing worse by the second.

Terran suddenly nodded his head, face firming with stubbornness, eyes reflecting resolve. Eyes that, Tam was relieved to see, had once again gone back to normal.

"Come on," Terran announced. "I need to make sure that weird scientist of yours is mixing up my medicine correctly."

Terran bounced off the way they had come. Tam trailed him, trying to resist the urge to throttle the little brat.

His mood shifted with sonic speed, though, when Tam spotted the large, red feather clinging tenaciously to Terran's back. He plucked it off, grinning. Tam twirled the bright plume in his fingers for a second before waving it in front of Terran's nose.

"You know, I should really be disturbed," he teased.

Terran made a face. "I was hungry," he said by way of explanation. "And bored."

Tam laughed, pocketing the feather. He steered Terran back to the clinic, past the now highly amused nurse, through the rear door and into the dingy combination warehouse and laboratory once more. Marvin huddled in his corner again, but a small, green bottle was displayed prominently on the metal table at his side.

Tam grinned. Marvin might be a jerk, not always completely trustworthy, incredibly scattered and more than a little frustrating, but there was no one better at solving puzzles. He'd charge you a fortune to do it, but Marvin always came through in the end.

Terran carefully tucked his precious bottle into the knapsack slung over his shoulder. He patted the cloth and smiled with relief.

"You done good, Marv," he announced.

"I live to serve," Marvin replied dryly. He pecked away at his keyboard, barely acknowledging their presence, mind already occupied with the next puzzle on his list.

"Come on," Tam said with a grin. "Marv doesn't even know we're here anymore."

"He needs a girlfriend," Terran said.

"I have one," Marv called over his shoulder. "She's a Lorothion fighter pilot and would eat you for breakfast."

"Cool," Terran commented. "Wait, do you mean figuratively or literally? Because I've heard some things about Lorothions—"

"Time to go," Tam interrupted, steering Terran towards the door with a firm grip on the little man's shoulder. Terran obediently went, waving a cheerful goodbye to the nurse on the way.

Terran jogged after Tam as they re-entered the bazaar. Rich smells and sounds smacked him in the face with the force of a blow. And what smells. Terran's stomach sang a loud chorus. *Oh, food.* He had taken his first dose of his medication and freely admitted that Marvin was a genius. He already felt much less distractible and less likely to fly off into la-la land at any second. But food? That was not a distraction. Terran had been much too jittery to eat earlier, and his last meal had been…way too long ago.

"Tam?" Terran panted, running a few steps to catch up with the big man. "I'm hungry."

"We'll get something back at the ship."

Terran wrinkled his nose. *Processor food. Ick.* Well, not really ick, but he wanted something real for a change. Like cooked in a kitchen real, not thawed out and zapped with microwave rays.

"Can't we stop somewhere?" he asked.

"No."

"But we have to eat sometime," Terran protested.

Tam stopped and heaved a sigh heavy enough to make his chest rise and fall noticeably. Hands on his hips, he stared at the ceiling several storeys above their heads.

Terran had seen his dad adopt that exact same pose dozens of times over the course of his lifetime. When he was about five, Terran had asked Evan Praetis what he was doing. His dad had sighed, too, and said, "Praying for guidance. And patience. Lots and lots of patience."

Terran had been a bit of a brat in his younger days. Of course, he had long since outgrown that phase. Really.

Terran smiled up at Tam's handsome face, twining their fingers together and donning his best hopeful smile. "I'm really, really hungry," he wheedled.

"How can you possibly be hungry?" Tam asked. "You ate your weight in pancakes this morning. Not to mention the parrot."

"The pancakes were *hours* ago. And I didn't eat the parrot." Terran wrinkled his nose in disgust. "That's just…ewww. I only played with it a bit. It made a really cool noise when it got freaked out."

Tam's lips twitched and he shook his head. "All right," he gave in, albeit with a distinct lack of grace.

Terran tugged on their joined hands to get Tam moving again. Apparently, he wasn't the only one who needed to eat. In the past few days, Terran had got to know Tam pretty well and had come to, well, rely on the man's easy-going nature. The current grumpy expression on his face would certainly be erased after a nice, solid meal.

They had only gone a few steps when Tam took over, which was good since Terran had no clue where he was going. It thrilled him, though, that Tam kept hold of his hand while they turned corners and wove through the sporadic crowds of people along the wide hallways.

They finally stopped in front of a red door, which was propped open with a little golden statue. Terran's nose twitched. *The smells, oh, the smells.* He followed Tam eagerly over the threshold and into a lush, rich world.

Just like at the clinic, the waiter greeted Tam with familiarity and showed them to a seat. Before long, they were being presented with a vast array of colourful items.

Terran drank deeply of the beverage Tam had ordered, trying to soothe the fiery burn from that last piece of meat. The smooth, fruity concoction coated his throat, providing some welcome relief.

"I want to try that one next," Terran said, pointing at a chicken dish smothered in some sort of orange sauce.

Tam's lips turned up at the corners, probably at Terran's enthusiasm, as he speared a piece of chicken with his fork. Instead of taking the utensil like he had last time, Terran leaned over and wrapped his lips around the offered food. He hummed happily at the explosion of flavours, letting the tines slip from his mouth. He sat back, licking his lips slowly. Seductively.

Okay, so he was flirting. Who could blame him? Tam was just so gorgeous. The large man's nostrils flared, eyes darkening, and Terran smirked with the first flush of success. *Oh, yeah.* He was definitely getting to the big mercenary.

An image flashed into his head, Tam and Dai leaning over Terran, smothering him with their big, hot bodies. Terran squirmed in his seat, reaching under the table to adjust himself as arousal hit, hard and powerful.

"Terran." Tam's voice held more than a hint of warning, his voice deeper than normal.

Terran ignored him. He licked his lips again and asked for another piece of chicken.

In response, Tam shoved the plate across the table to Terran. *Spoilsport.*

Terran rallied quickly at the slight rebuff. He was busy planning his next attack when Tam spoke.

"We should head back soon. Daior will be waking up before long, and I don't want him to be alone when he does. Knowing Dai, he'd try to 'escape' the ship and then we'd have to waste our time tracking him down."

Terran sat up straighter, hearing that tone in Tam's voice again. The one that always appeared whenever Tam mentioned Daior. "Did you and him have a thing?" he asked. "You know, a relationship? Because Dai got really cranky when your name came up."

"Daior's always cranky."

Terran rolled his eyes. "Different kind of cranky," he declared. "The kind that usually means some kind of history."

Tam dipped his head, but not before Terran saw the sadness that turned the man's light blue eyes nearly colourless.

"It was a long time ago," Tam insisted, poking half-heartedly at the remains of his meal. "And it didn't end well."

The sadness slipped away, a hard, remote expression taking its place. Terran wanted to curse. How the heck had they ended up so serious? Until now, they'd been having a wonderful time, talking and laughing and sharing food. And flirting. Or at least Terran had been flirting. Terran wanted to smack himself upside the head. He just couldn't resist prodding, could he?

"So…"

"We should go." Tam signalled for their waiter.

Terran suppressed a groan. "I'm not finished," he protested.

Amusement flickered across Tam's face, lightening Terran's spirit.

Tam surveyed the piles of mostly empty plates scattered across the table, and his mouth twisted into a wry smile. "I think we emptied the kitchen," he commented. "You eat any more and I'll have to roll you out of here. Where the hell does someone your size put all that food?"

"I need a lot of energy." Terran tried for a suggestive smirk, but Tam didn't take the hint. The big mercenary just shook his head, handing over his bank card to the waiter.

The waiter almost dropped the card, eyes going wide with shock, when Terran asked for take-home containers. Tam nearly choked on his laughter.

Terran just shrugged. He was used to the reaction. What could he say? He was a growing boy. Still. Always.

Loaded down with goodies, they exited the cool interior of the restaurant and stepped out into the much warmer air of the Station corridors. The hour was growing late, but people still bustled about purposefully. The Stations never really shut down. With ships constantly arriving and departing—and no sun or moon to demarcate days—many businesses never closed. In many ways, it reminded Terran of his brother's ship. Voyagers were huge, capable of hosting several hundred crew members comfortably for years at a time in deep space. Like the Stations, people were always around and the days seemed to meld into each other.

When Terran had first gone into space, he'd found the constant activity exciting. Now, it grated a bit. He was actually looking forward to getting back to the quiet and solitude of the *Farion*. It hadn't taken long for the small cruiser to begin feeling like home. More like home, in fact, than Richard's massive floating fortress had ever felt. And Terran had lived on the *Celsius* for years.

They passed another intersection, the steel hallways that marched off in four directions all looking alike to Terran. A group of people clustered around the tiny map screen hanging on the wall, but Tam didn't pay it any attention. It was that action alone that told Terran exactly how much time Tam must have spent on Indara. Space Stations tended to grow, additional decks being added to the top and bottom, hallways growing outwards. The practice tended to turn the Stations into confusing labyrinths after a while, impenetrable to all but those who made the Station their permanent home. Terran would have been utterly lost in seconds, and he wasn't too proud to admit it. He didn't see a single recognisable landmark as they navigated the maze of corridors and floating walkways, but suddenly they were passing under the archway leading to the main docking area.

The familiar grey-blue hull of the *Farion* entered their view, and Terran made his move. A shove caught Tam off guard, and Terran seized the opportunity to push the large man up against the wall, managing it only because of the element of surprise. Terran's pack and his bag of leftovers hit the ground as he wrapped one hand around Tam's arm. Terran stood on top of the man's thick boots, but it still wasn't enough height, so he grabbed Tam's long braid with his free hand. He still had to half crawl up the large, hard body as he used Tam's hair to pull the man's head down to meet his own. Terran caught Tam's lips, teasing and sliding his own over them.

"Wait, what?" Tam stiffened for a moment, then instinct took over. One of those lovely, strong arms wrapped around Terran's waist and hauled him up. Terran draped both arms around Tam's neck and threw himself heart and soul into the kiss.

Terran let himself wallow in the embrace, loving the difference between Tam and Daior. Where Dai was domination and demands, Tam was persuasion and seduction. Both men kissed like gods, and Terran would happily spend the rest of his life exploring the differences and similarities in styles.

Tam moaned, and Terran's thoughts vanished into a morass of lust. The gentle brush of lips, the searching tongue. It was a give and take, an exchange of emotions. Terran relished the feel of hard muscles cradling him close, the large hand caressing him. Tam teased at the roof of Terran's mouth with his tongue, and Terran opened wider, inviting his big soon-to-be-lover to take everything he wanted.

With shocking abruptness, Terran's world dropped out from under him. Literally. Terran staggered as his feet hit the ground, and he looked up into a pair of blue eyes dark with dismay.

"We—" Tam broke off, voice hoarse. He licked his lips and tried again. "We can't do this, Terran. What about Daior?"

"I—"

"This is wrong, and you know it," Tam insisted. "We can't do this. *I* can't do this. I can't hurt Daior like that."

Terran opened his mouth to explain, protest, anything, but the words would have been spoken to himself. Tam fled with agitated strides, back stiff and unyielding, distress written in every line of his bulky frame.

*Well, damn.* That hadn't gone at all as planned.

Terran gathered up his bags, chewing on his lower lip and trying not to feel devastated by Tam's rejection. His arousal had faded quickly, now a distant memory. He followed Tam onto the *Farion,* trying to figure out why everything had gone so horribly wrong.

Maybe Richard was right. Terran really couldn't survive in regular society. There were just so many times that Terran couldn't understand his fellow humans. They had such strange notions. So many restrictions and unspoken rules, he mused. Terran shoved his food and medication into the small galley refrigerator with a bit more force than necessary.

*Cheating?* Hurt vied with anger at Tam's implied accusation. He wasn't cheating on Daior. He wouldn't. Terran might be far more used to one-night stands than relationships, but he was always faithful. Always. Terran just happened to believe you could be faithful to more than one person at a time. That a relationship didn't have to revolve around just two people.

He sighed, munching absently on a leftover roll snagged from one of the containers he'd brought back with him. It was probably the cat in him. Terran had read somewhere that a male cat tended to surround himself with a little pack of females, making the rounds when he felt the need. Terran happened to pick males, but the theory was the same.

He just couldn't see what was wrong with wanting Tam. The attraction he felt towards the blond-headed Viking throwback was as strong as the attraction he felt for his Daior. There was more than enough of Terran to go around. Not only that, but the two mercenaries had a past together, caring that was still evident in both of them. The three of them together could have something really special, Terran just knew it.

Terran had a sudden, nearly overwhelming urge to call his mother. She could always make him feel better. It was her wisdom and understanding that had got him through those first horrible years right after puberty when the cat part of his DNA had surged, turning the world upside down and inside out.

Every time Terran had thought he was managing to fit in, figuring out normal human behaviour, something like his current mess would pop up. Something that had proved Terran wasn't quite right and never would be. He supposed glumly that he should really just resign himself to living the rest of his life as a freak.

He really didn't know what to do next. It was a feeling he was used to, and he certainly didn't like it. At a complete loss, he wandered to the front of the ship. Tam was setting the controls and clearing their takeoff with the Dock Master, so Terran hovered in the door until the conversation concluded before entering the cabin.

"What do you want, Terran?" Tam didn't turn around.

*Well, hell.* Terran hated when people were mad at him. *Hated* it.

"I'm sorry," he choked out, staring at the floor, not really sure what he was apologising for. "It's just, I really like you."

"And what about Daior?" Tam responded harshly.

"I like him, too. I like both of you. I want both of you."

"That's not how it works!" Tam let his head drop forward and sighed. When he spoke again, his voice was gentler but no less firm. "You can't have it that way, Terran. I'll help you figure out who kidnapped you, how to get them to go away. And you'll always have my friendship. But please, don't push. I'm not sure I'm strong enough to resist. Daior claimed you first, and I'm not going to mess with that."

Terran gnawed on his lower lip some more as Tam turned his attention back to the ship's controls, clearly done with the conversation.

Well, so was Terran. There wasn't much more to say, was there? Terran did something uncharacteristic. He fled.

Back in his room, he flopped down onto the bed, covered his face with his hands and let loose with a frustrated scream.

The outlet drained some of his anger, leaving behind an overwhelming feeling of exhaustion. Maybe things would be clearer when Daior woke up. Terran just really, really hoped that was soon. Maybe then he could convince both men that what they could have together was right.

Besides, if this dragged on much longer? Well, Terran wasn't quite certain he would be able to honour Tam's request. Everything inside him screamed that Terran was meant to have both of his big men. He had a little problem of single-mindedness when there was something he wanted. That, and a lack of willpower.

Terran yanked a blanket over his head and curled up. A nap. He'd feel much better after a nap. And who knew, maybe some brilliant solution would occur to him while he slept.

*One could always hope.*

Terran slipped off to sleep with visions of Tam and Daior locked in an embrace dancing across his imagination.

# Chapter Eleven

Daior sat up with a groan, reflexively grabbing his head with both hands. Damn, how many Agrarian Chasers had he downed?

*Oh, yeah. None.* He growled. No alcohol. No hangover. Just a bunch of walking dead men. When he got his hands on those guards…

*Terran.* Where the hell was his Terran?

He leapt off the table, staggering sideways when his feet hit the metal floor. *Ah, cold.* He took two unsteady steps before he realised something was missing.

Clothes. He needed clothes. Couldn't wander a strange ship buck naked. Might not go over so well.

Daior let out a few curses and started rummaging. He slammed an empty drawer shut and winced when the sound made his head throb. It felt as if somebody had shoved a wad of cotton balls up his nose and stuck a pick into the base of his neck. Bloody sadistic bastard, whoever it was.

Dai went through three drawers before he saw the neatly folded pile on a chair by the door. Shit, he must be worse off than he'd first thought. He was normally a lot more observant than that.

By the time he had pulled on the loose-fitting pants and tied the drawstring around his hips, his head had cleared out a bit. Still hurt like a son of a bitch, but at least he felt a bit more…functioning.

He slapped his hand against the door panel, half-expecting it to be locked. He was pleased when it hissed open easily. *So, friends.* Whatever vessel he was on, it was owned by friends.

Despite that conclusion, Dai still entered the hall with caution. First order of business—find Terran. Second—find out where the hell they were.

His head hurt too much to count any higher.

The door to the med bay closed behind him and Dai looked around. The hallway only went one way, which made things considerably easier for his poor, pounding brain. He took a couple of steps, pleased to note his legs seemed to be working much better now.

Laughter floated down the hall, ricocheting off the walls and reaching his ears oddly fractured. Daior flattened himself against the cold metal, muscles tensing. Wait, there was something familiar about…both of them.

A fierce scowl immediately replaced his battle tension. *Tamesis. Damn the man.* If Tam had made a move on Dai's baby, someone was going to be missing some vital parts by this evening. And it wasn't going to be Dai.

Daior ignored the little voice taunting him and moved to the centre of the hallway, planting himself with the immovability of a wall and folding his arms over his chest.

Terran and Tamesis came around the corner. Terran hung off the larger man's arm with the tenacity of a monkey, body shaking with giggles.

"Explanation, anyone?" Daior drawled.

Terran squealed—ear-piercing, that—and flung himself across the space between them. Dai grinned as the smaller man tried to climb up his body.

"You okay, baby?" he asked.

"Oh, Gods, Dai. I thought you weren't ever going to wake up. It's been days and days, and we kept having to jump through holes, and—"

"Let the man breathe," Tam ordered with an indulgent smile.

"Mind your own business," Dai said.

The smile slid off Tam's face. Without a word, he turned on his heel and disappeared the way he had come.

Terran pulled back, still hanging onto Dai's neck. "That wasn't very nice," he scolded gently.

"I'm not feeling very nice," Dai retorted. "My head is pounding, my back feels like someone shoved a pole up my spine, my lover is wrapped all over a man I despise and I haven't the slightest clue where we are or what's going on!"

"There's no need to yell."

"I'll yell if I want to."

"You weren't nearly this cranky when we were being held prisoner," Terran accused.

Dai sighed heavily and hugged the lithe body to him. "Sorry. I'm just a little on edge right now."

"We're safe," Terran assured him. "Tam got us both out of there. We've been galaxy hopping, trying to stay a few steps ahead of the cruisers the compound sent after us. For a place that wasn't very well guarded inside, they sure have a lot of artillery in space."

"Big backing, then."

"That's what Tam said."

Daior ran his fingers through that spiky hair. "I'm glad you're okay, baby."

"Same here." Terran smiled. "I missed you."

"How long was I out?"

"Nearly a week."

"Shit," Dai said with intense feeling.

"We've covered a lot of ground—or rather, space—in that time." Terran grabbed his hand. "Come on. Let's go find Tam. We have a lot to talk about."

Dai didn't move, pulling Terran to a halt when their arms reached their limits between them. He was scowling again. "Just get your stuff together. There's no need to involve Tamesis in this any further."

Terran yanked himself free and planted his hands on his hips, lips pressing together in a stubborn pout. "Now you're being ridiculous. I don't know what went on between you two, but Tam is already involved. You did that the minute you called him. They're after him as much as they're after us now. I'm not abandoning him."

*Hell.* Maybe Daior should just go back to sleep.

"Terran—"

"No! I like the man. And he's risked a lot to help us. So go make nice."

*Damn it.* He really wasn't up to this argument. Maybe when his head stopped pounding.

*Nah, probably not then, either.*

"Terran—"

"You're not going to win this argument. You might as well accept that right now."

Who knew a face that, well, pretty could look so mulish.

Daior dragged one hand down his own face. "You think you could find me something to eat, baby?"

Obstinacy morphed into concern. "Of course. What do you want?"

"Food."

"Right." Terran grabbed his hand and started tugging again. Dai followed his lover down the corridor. When the way split, Terran pushed him to the right.

"Bridge is that way," he offered cheerfully. "Food is this way. I'll get you something to eat and meet you up front."

Terran stopped mid-bounce to press a kiss to Daior's cheek. That wasn't good enough for Daior. He turned his head and pulled Terran into a toe-curling, tongue-involved expression of passion and longing.

When they came up for air, Terran smiled at him. His eyes were a bit dreamy around the edges, his smile about the best thing Daior had seen in ages.

"I'm glad you're awake," Terran offered, his smile softening.

Daior really wasn't ready to analyse the emotion he glimpsed there. Maybe when his thinking cleared. Then again, maybe not.

Daior watched that pert arse disappear around the corner. His own smile slowly slid off his face. *Best get this over with.* He had a feeling Terran wouldn't leave him alone until he did. Hell, the man might even withhold Dai's food. And Daior really needed food.

The corridor dead-ended in a door that slid open with a near-silent hiss when Daior approached. He paused in the entrance, impressed despite his foul mood. Seemed Tam had done pretty well for himself over the last decade. The ship appeared sleek and well-designed from the inside, the curved screens marching along in front of him high quality. Although small, the bridge gleamed with care and displayed some expensive navigation equipment.

Tam slouched in one of the seats. He'd swivelled it sideways and stared with unseeing eyes at the wall, legs sprawling wide and bumping into the co-pilot's chair.

"Tamesis."

The blond head came up, eyes uncertain. "Daior."

Dai leaned against the entryway, ignoring the way the door kept trying to close into his shoulder. "I suppose I owe you a thanks."

"No, you don't," Tam replied sharply.

"Well, you're getting it, anyway."

"You're welcome."

Uncomfortable silence settled over the room. Tam broke first.

"Where's Terran?"

"I sent him for food."

"Yeah, I imagine you're starving. It took some work, getting all your systems up and running. I didn't know you...we...could suppress them that long."

"You can do a lot of things if you're desperate enough."

"You mean stubborn enough."

"I never claimed to be anything else."

Tam shot to his feet and planted his hands on his hips. "Damn it, Daior, what the hell do you want me to say?"

"You could start with an apology."

"For what?" Tam's cheeks were gaining a hint of ruddy colour, a sure sign his temper was slipping. He was usually the cool-headed one of the pair, at least back in the day, but Tam could blow with the best of them. Or the worst. Whichever.

"You know for what."

"That was ten years ago!"

Daior fixed his coldest stare on his former best friend, partner and lover. Tam held his gaze for several seconds before looking away.

"All right," he said. "I'm sorry."

Daior nodded once, knowing the motion was arrogant and would annoy the hell out of Tamesis.

Or at least, it would have annoyed the old Tamesis. This one just looked sad. Maybe some things changed, after all. The thought was rather disconcerting.

"Where are we?" Daior asked. He wandered over to the console and pulled up the most recent map.

"We just left Indara."

"So the best drop site would probably be—"

"You don't have to go anywhere," Tam interrupted. "Keeping on the move is the safest course, right now. Whoever these guys are, they've got money and connections."

Daior didn't look up from his maps. "No, thanks," he said, voice icy. "I can take care of Terran just fine by myself."

He didn't turn around, but Tam's form reflected clearly in the glass video screens along the front of the ship. Powered off and dark, they worked just as good as any mirror.

"I can't convince you to—"

"No."

Something in either voice or posture must have convinced Tamesis. The man sort of…deflated. His shoulders dropped and he turned away. "I'll just…"

"Why did you come?" Daior couldn't resist asking.

Shoulders hunched, muscles tense, Tamesis paused with his back still to Daior. "What are you talking about?"

"To get us, when I called. Why did you come?"

Tam's eyes slid shut. Damn it, the man shouldn't even have to ask. That he did…

"Forget it," he said gruffly, still without turning. He didn't want Dai to see the pain in his eyes, the pain he knew he wouldn't be able to hide.

"I can't."

"So, you wouldn't have come? If I had called *you* for help?"

He regretted the question as soon as it left his lips. Daior's hesitation was more truth than he wanted at the moment.

"Never mind," he growled. "We'll head back to Indara. I can draw them off you and Terran for a while."

"Tam—"

"Please, Dai. Don't."

He remembered the last time he'd begged this man for something. It hadn't worked then, either.

"Damn it, Tamesis! Stop being such a gods-damn martyr."

Tam's temper suddenly snapped. He whirled. "You were the one who ended it, remember? Don't get all righteous on me now."

"And I still think I did the right thing," Dai insisted. He stepped forward until they were almost nose to nose.

Tam wanted to wince at the anger on the face of the man who had once been his entire universe.

"It wasn't working anymore," Dai continued. "We weren't working anymore."

"But you didn't even try!"

"The hell I didn't!" Daior bellowed back. "I did everything short of re-programming myself. And not even you were worth that."

"Did I ever ask you to go that far? I would have taken whatever you chose to give me," Tamesis insisted hoarsely.

"Selective memory much? Or don't you remember that last fight? We nearly killed each other."

"I didn't mean it."

"Well, neither did I. But it doesn't change reality. We're too much alike to ever make it work. And I've moved on."

*Terran. Black hole take it.* The only man Tam had ever met that he wanted as much as he wanted Dai. And he couldn't have either one of them.

Sometimes life was just so blasted unfair.

Tam sighed. He hated this, hated fighting with this man. Always had, always would. But it was inevitable. Daior knew exactly which emotional buttons to push. He didn't do it on purpose, Tam knew that. Didn't help, though.

Dai's expression altered, some of the anger fading. "Look, I'll take Terran and go. When I'm not here, you can go back to your life. Move on again."

"I never moved on."

Tam could have bitten off his tongue, immediately wanting to call the words back. Dai studied him with fascination, like a collector with a unique specimen. Tam knew the desperation on his face spoke louder than the words, and those screamed bloody murder.

*Well, hell.* As the old Earth saying went, in for a penny, in for a pound. He'd never understood the details of that one, but the meaning fit.

"You were it for me," Tam admitted. "You were always it for me."

Tam could feel the flush rise on his face, knew his cheeks were turning a dull red with embarrassment as Daior's mouth dropped open.

Then Dai's eyes lit with an all-too-familiar look of possession.

Dai lunged, reaching up to wrap his hands around Tam's shoulders, yanking Tam's lips down on his own. Gods, the man even tasted the same. A sweet mixture of honey and musk, lips warms and pliable, moving with such familiarity over his.

Tam jerked away with a gasp. "What the hell do you think you're doing?"

"Thought it was pretty obvious."

Tam wanted nothing more than to dive right back into that blistering kiss. But if he let this get any farther out of control, it was going to hurt even more than it did now.

"You've moved on, remember?" Tam pointed out.

A low moan had their heads swivelling in unison. Terran stood in the doorway, eyes shining with lust.

"Damn it," Dai said with a great deal of feeling.

"Oh, Gods, that was so hot," Terran said, licking his lips.

Dai's eyes practically bugged in shock. Tam figured he had a similar stupefied expression on his face. Of all the things he had expected to hear, that one hadn't even registered on his mental radar. It wasn't the usual reaction when someone caught their lover kissing another guy.

Of course, Tam had given up yesterday on trying to predict anything when it came to Terran. And after the whole parrot incident…well, nothing should surprise him anymore when it came to the little man.

Shouldn't. Still did.

Terran grinned. "Hamburger?" He thrust the plate at the room in general.

"Aren't you angry?" Dai asked. He took the plate of food automatically but didn't seem to see it. All his focus was on the smaller man watching them with big, blue eyes.

"No," Terran said, snagging a fry. "Makes things easier on me. Now I don't have to choose."

"Choose?" Daior still did growly really well.

"We're gonna talk *now*?" And Terran did whiney really well.

Terran sighed heavily and dramatically, donning his best put-upon face. "I care about both of you. A lot. It was driving me nuts. I don't want to have to pick one or the other. I want you both. Maybe I'm selfish, but I don't think a person can ever have enough love. Besides, it will take both of you to keep up with me."

Terran waggled his eyebrows suggestively. Tam's muffled laugh came out as a quiet snort. Little Bit had a point there. If he caused so much mischief when he wasn't feeling the best, how bad would it be when the medicine started working? Tam had a vision of a kitten rocketing off furniture.

Despite his practical side trying to rear its ugly head, Tam couldn't suppress a surge of hope.

One look at Daior's face, and that hope died a swift, brutal death.

Tam mumbled something, not even sure what he said. He brushed past Terran, ignoring the squeaked protest, and fled.

# Chapter Twelve

Terran watched Tam leave and his feet twitched in his leather boots, wanting to run after the man and wrap him up in a big hug. Tam had just looked so miserable.

"You're being mean again," Terran scolded.

"What?" Dai asked with a scowl. "I didn't say anything."

"You didn't have to."

Dai grabbed his hamburger and devoured half in one bite. The scowl on his face didn't invite further conversation.

Terran ignored the forbidding expression. "You're being an ass."

Daior choked.

Terran rushed over and smacked Dai on the back a couple of times. Hard. Terran pressed his lips together tightly and donned his best study-in-annoyance face. He'd learnt it in an art class. Not that he had the least bit of artistic talent. No, Terran had been the nude model. Fun times had been had by all. At least until his brother had found out. Killjoy.

"Terran."

Daior's warning made Terran want to arch his back and growl.

"No, you listen to me," Terran demanded. "Did you know you talk in your sleep?"

"The hell I do!"

"Okay, maybe not talk. You sort of mumble when you're half asleep. You called me Tam."

"I did not." Dai's voice didn't hold much conviction.

"Did too."

"Terran."

"Would you stop saying my name like that? I'm not a child."

"I know you're not."

Dai tried to leer at him. Terran smacked him on the shoulder.

"Not now, I'm trying to get something to stick in that thick head of yours."

"Baby, I just woke up. My head is pounding, I ache and this burger wasn't nearly enough to kill the hunger."

"Sorry," Terran said, feeling contrite at the reminder. But that didn't mean he was going to give up. He had a feeling if he let the matter drop, he wouldn't get another chance. "But I need you to listen to me."

"We tried it once," Dai said quietly.

Terran snapped his mouth shut when he realised Dai was actually talking to him. Not just saying words, but sharing.

"Tam and I grew up together. We were specifically designed to work together, fight together. For years we were partners. And lovers. But it didn't work out.

We're too much alike. I've moved on. Whatever feelings I had for Tam are in the past, and that's where they're going to stay."

"But I don't think they are in the past." Terran was deadly serious as he tugged Dai around to look at him. "Whatever you felt for Tam is still there. And I want to be a part of it. You just said you guys were made for each other."

"Professionally."

"Same difference. Maybe it didn't work before, but you have me now. I can be your gooey centre, keep you guys from going all macho on each other. Dai, please."

Dai was going to refuse. Terran could see it on his face.

"I don't understand what the problem is," Terran protested.

"Life isn't that simple."

Terran rolled his eyes. "Trite, Daior. I don't see why not. What's so complicated? I like both of you. You like each other. Why can't we all have what we want?"

"Terran—"

Terran scowled at the bigger man, not understanding why Dai was having so much trouble with this current idea. It was an inspired plan, if he did say so himself. And he did. All of his plans were inspired.

Well, maybe not all. There was that one time with the new food processor and…never mind. Maybe that idea hadn't been inspired, but this one most definitely was.

"Terran, can we please talk about this later?" Dai held up one hand when Terran started to protest. "I swear we will. When my head isn't splitting in two and my stomach isn't trying to gnaw its way to the kitchen. All right?"

*Not really.* Terran wanted this settled, and now. But…Dai *was* looking kind of pale and pinched.

His nurturing side kicked in. "All right," he agreed. He took Dai's arm, tugging him gently towards the door. "Let's get some more food in you. Then I'll tuck you into bed for a while."

"You'll join me?"

"Where else would I be?" Terran replied seriously. Then he smiled with all the glee of a mischievous imp. "Besides, you need to relax. And I know the perfect relaxation technique."

"Massage?" Daior asked hopefully.

Terran laughed. "I clearly haven't corrupted you enough."

"No massage?"

"I've got something better in mind than a massage," Terran promised. He flashed his best wicked grin.

Daior's clearly still fuzzy mind caught on. "I suppose that'll do," he teased.

Terran whacked him lightly on the arm and resisted the childish urge to stick out his tongue.

After another two hamburgers, Daior willingly followed Terran back down the corridor and to the bedroom Terran had been using over the last week. It was large for such a tiny ship, but then said ship had clearly been remodelled extensively. In a reflection of Indara, the normally sterile, utilitarian décor had been remodelled, too. Thick rugs in vibrant reds, purples and golds were strewn along the floor, sucking up some of the cold that could never quite be eradicated from the metal, no matter how many heating coils were run underneath. Equally vibrant cloths in a mix of silky and sheer material draped the walls in pleasing cascades. The half of the room nearest to the door had been turned into a small office-relaxation area. Two plush chairs, a desk and a tiny entertainment console were arranged haphazardly on a raised platform. Down a pair of steps brought them into the main bedroom.

The bed itself was a massive affair, taking up nearly the entire middle of the room. A far cry from the normal hard mattresses that were always either too narrow or too short, this bed was soft and squishy and covered in big, fluffy pillows. They made a fantastic nest.

Terran shoved Daior backwards onto the bed, grinning in pleasure as the bigger man dropped. They'd explore the bathroom later, when they had a bit more need of it. Like the room, it was lovely and decadent and Terran couldn't wait to introduce Dai to the joys of multiple showerheads.

Well, actually, he could wait. There was something Terran wanted to do first.

He resisted the urge to pout some more. "Up," he ordered sternly.

Daior cracked an eyelid at him. "Already there. I'm not *that* tired."

Terran snickered. "Not quite what I meant."

Dai propped himself against the pillows with a low groan. "I feel like someone ran me over with an old-style steamroller."

"I don't know what that means, but it sounds painful."

"Very."

Terran crawled up the covers, planted both hands on Daior's thighs and leaned in for a kiss. "Just relax," he said against the firm lips. He could still taste the burgers Dai had eaten mixed in with the taste of his man. "I'll take care of everything."

"I like the sound of that."

Terran stripped off his shirt and tossed it over his shoulder. Dai reached for Terran's nipples as if his hands were pulled by magnets. Terran groaned. "For you," he stated firmly.

"This *is* for me." Daior tweaked the tight buds, grinning with open humour.

Terran shoved Daior's hands aside long enough to get the man bared to the waist. While he went to work on yanking Dai's pants down, Dai busied himself stroking Terran's shoulders and laying a trail of wet, open-mouthed kisses to the side of his neck.

Terran wriggled. "Slow down," he scolded. "You don't feel well."

"Mmm. Feeling better by the second."

As that was kind of the point, Terran kept going. When he'd managed to get them both naked, he plopped himself in Dai's lap.

"Careful," Dai warned.

"Stop worrying. As if I'd damage my favourite body part."

"Gee, nice to know you love me for my brain," Daior replied dryly.

"You shouldn't be able to think this much," Terran informed him. "I guess I'll just have to work harder."

Dai gasped, dropping his head back as Terran slithered down the mattress. Dai let his body follow his head a second later, and he collapsed onto the bed. "Lord, baby."

Terran smiled. He teased a bit, rubbing his hands along Daior's hips. He buried his face against Dai's chiselled stomach, surrounding himself with the musky scent of his lover, just breathing against the skin. Dai groaned and Terran smiled wider. Warm breath against sensitive flesh could be surprisingly arousing, if done right. And when it came to sex, Terran knew how to do it right.

Daior's muscles were rock hard beneath Terran's touch, and a small furrow was deepening between his brows. *Time to speed things up.* A little rush of endorphins to dull the pain, let Daior go back to sleep. *Yeah, just what the doctor ordered.* Or would have, if he'd been here. Or maybe not. But he should.

Terran reined in his rambling thoughts with the best possible distraction. He swooped down, opening wide and sliding his lips over the head of Daior's cock. He licked off a few drops of pre-cum to ease the way, bobbing shallowly.

Then he really started showing off. Terran closed his lips around Dai, pulling back far enough to swirl around the head with his tongue before he took in more of the thick cock. He tilted his head, held his breath and opened his throat. Dai shouted and bucked. Terran was prepared, hands holding Dai's hips still to keep himself from choking. He held there for a minute, massaging Dai with his throat.

Damn, but he loved this. Terran purred around the hard heat in his mouth, sliding off for another taste of the crown before taking in the smooth skin of Dai's shaft again. He soon had a steady rhythm going. Up and down, up and swirl with the tongue, back down. Dai writhed and wriggled underneath him, a song of moans filling the air in tandem with Terran's movements. Terran's own body was enjoying the rhythm, as well. He lay atop one sturdy, hairy leg, pressing his own throbbing cock against Dai's calf, humping while he sucked.

"Close, baby," Daior gasped. He wound his fingers in Terran's hair, stroking and tugging, as if making sure Terran didn't get away.

As if Terran had any intention at all of going anywhere. Coming, yes. Going, no.

Terran pulled back, letting Daior's cock slip reluctantly from his mouth. "Anytime, lover," he encouraged.

Daior bit out a curse, trying to pull Terran's head back to his dick. "Don't stop now, brat!"

Terran ignored the order. He hadn't quite finished exploring, now, had he? Had to make sure everything was still in working order, don't you know. He spent long minutes examining the base of Daior's cock. Thick and hard, curving upwards just slightly. He traced a vein with one finger, circling the hard column with his other hand.

"So pretty," he murmured.

"Baby, nothing about me is pretty."

Maybe not pretty, but Terran definitely liked. He dipped his head, following the trail of scent from the tip of Daior's cock—nice and strong, pre-cum oozing steadily from the slit—lower as it lessened, then down farther into Dai's tight balls, where the smell grew stronger again. He licked and suckled gently, pulling more of those lovely moans and groans from Daior. Terran's skin felt hot, flushed, and he lipped Dai's tight sac gently before nipping, not quite so gently. He snaked one hand around to cup Daior's balls, exploring with his fingers as he followed Daior's urging for his mouth to return to the man's cock.

Daior's erection actually looked painful now. Terran hummed in sympathy, kissing the tip to make it better.

"Terran!"

Terran started up his rhythm again and continued in his apparent quest to drive Dai insane. Terran rubbed his fingers firmly against the skin behind Daior's balls, edging near to the heat of his arse before backing off. He stroked that path, balls to arse, back and forth, head bobbing faster and faster.

Daior practically screamed his name, body surging upwards as he came in a nearly violent explosion. Terran pulled back, letting the creamy spunk hit his tongue, savouring the taste. He sucked deeply, trying to keep up with his lover's release, but a bit leaked from his lips where they were sealed as tightly as he could get them around Daior.

Dai's muscles relaxed with the last ejaculation, body going limp. "Damn." His voice was hoarse, exhausted.

Terran pulled back and licked his lips, arousal hitting him hard and suddenly. Bucking against Daior's thigh, he whimpered. *Isn't enough.* He launched himself up, claiming a deep kiss, Dai's stubble abrading his cheeks, throbbing erection pinned between their bodies.

"Need," he begged.

Daior hushed him, one big hand reaching down to tug with harsh, rough motions at Terran's cock. It was just what Terran sought, relief surging through him even as his body hovered painfully on the edge of orgasm. Daior pulled him into another passionate kiss, teeth and lips and tongue clashing together. It wasn't gentle or seductive, just pure heat and need. Dai kept moving his hand. It felt as if he literally pulled Terran's climax from his cock.

Terran's mouth opened on a soundless cry, his orgasm sweeping over him so suddenly it stole his breath, leaving him able to do little more than hang on to the only solid thing in his world. His vision actually greyed out a bit at the edges as he clung to Dai. Their mouths were still locked together, but Terran had stopped participating. He just held there, lips open, submitting to whatever Daior desired.

His release seemed to go on forever, everything tight and hot and oh, so good. With a tiny cry, more of a loud exhale, really, Terran's muscles gave out. He dropped onto Daior's chest, panting hard, lungs struggling for air.

He couldn't move. All done in. Would just stay here for the next few days. *Yeah, good plan.*

Unfortunately, he had landed in a sticky puddle of his own cum. Not that Terran minded cum but, yeah, well, sticky. And getting cold.

Terran finally shoved himself off, grimacing.

Below him, Daior's eyes were closed, the man's chest moving evenly as he hovered on the verge of sleep.

If Terran could pat himself on the back, he would. Well, he could, but it would look a little silly, so he settled for a satisfied nod. *Relaxed, melty Daior. Goal achieved.*

Terran swung his feet onto the rug. It took him two tries to get his shaky legs to hold his weight, and the room seemed much larger than usual. He went into the bathroom then made his unsteady way back to the bed with a damp towel and wiped them both down, just enough to get rid of the sticky. The rag got tossed into a corner, and Terran dropped face-down onto the mattress beside Daior's big body.

That lasted for all of thirty seconds, then he rolled over. "I'm cold. Snuggle with me?"

Daior groaned but stretched out his arm and tucked Terran closer. "You are the snuggliest person I've ever come across."

"I like a good snuggle. See? I'm very demanding and spoilt, and you're going to have trouble keeping me satisfied." He made the proclamation with the air of a great decree, nodding once at the end for emphasis.

Daior cracked one eye open and glared balefully. "Your point being?"

"No one person can ever keep up with me," he assured Daior.

Dai sighed. "Are we back to this again? Please, Terran, can't it wait for morning?"

"We're in space," Terran pointed out. "There is no morning."

Dai groaned, head dropping back on the pillows. He closed his eyes, muttering something inaudible.

"I'm trouble," Terran agreed solemnly. He would make his point yet, yes, he would. Daior wasn't stupid. Dense sometimes, but not stupid. The big man would come around. Terran was just impatient. Very impatient. Insanely impatient.

Really, really bad at waiting for good stuff.

"That you are. Go to sleep."

Terran wriggled around until he pretty much sprawled on top of Dai's warm, firm chest. He settled in for his second favourite pastime, napping. He would even be good and actually nap.

Terran propped his chin on Daior's chest. "I'm still cold." He grinned when he said it, though, and Dai caught on right away. His big mercenary sighed heavily and closed his eyes, dragging Terran firmly against him, the unspoken message quite clear. The spoken one, too.

"No, you're a brat."

"But I'm your brat."

The slight smile that lightened the grouchy face told Terran a lot. It wasn't necessarily that Dai was against the idea of all three of them. He was just against the idea of Terran preferring Tam over him.

Well, that wasn't going to happen. Terran figured, though, that only time would prove how important *both* men were to him. Now he just had to figure out a way to get the time he needed.

He figured sex. Sex was always a really good persuader. Seriously, he was like the cutest thing ever. How could either of the stubborn idiots resist?

# Chapter Thirteen

Amazingly well, as it turned out. Terran considered throwing something at the nearest wall out of sheer frustration. So far, Operation Threesome had completely stalled. Both Dai and Tam were avoiding him. And each other. They argued constantly, over everything from the colour of the nearest star to their next destination. Heck, Terran had even heard them arguing over the merits of waffles versus pancakes for breakfast.

And in the meantime, Terran wasn't getting any. No touching, no kissing and most definitely no sex. It was making him itchy. He wasn't used to going without for very long, particularly when there were two such gorgeous male specimens within range.

Terran sprawled on the bed in Dai's quarters, flicking little bits of lint off the dark grey bedspread. *Bored.* He was so bored. And out of ideas. He needed a plan. A brilliant, unique plan that would have both men falling into bed with him.

He sighed heavily and flopped over onto his back, staring at the ceiling.

Restlessness was a living creature wrapping around his spine. Terran rolled over again and propped his head on his elbow, looking across the room at Dai. His lover was bent over the big wooden desk on the other side of the doorway, doing much too good a job of ignoring Terran.

Terran took a moment to admire the hunky form. Dai had shaved off the beard and it made a huge improvement in his looks, if Terran did say so himself. Not that Terran was against facial hair. He thought Tam's beard was absolutely luscious. Dai, however, just looked fuzzy. Without the dark stubble, Terran could see the firm jaw, the cleft in Dai's strong chin. It made him want to run his tongue all over that tanned skin.

"Dai?" Terran called.

"Hmmm?" The other man didn't even bother to look up from his work.

Oh, that just wouldn't do at all.

"Daior!"

"What?" Dai looked up with clear irritation.

"Whatcha doin'?"

"Contemplating murder," came the muttered reply.

"Come on, I've been good for hours. I'm bored. Talk to me."

"I don't talk."

"Then why are there words coming out of your mouth?"

Dai tossed his pen down. "Fine, brat. What do you want?"

"I was just thinking."

"Gods help us all."

Terran ignored the comment with practised ease. "Why did the guys who kidnapped me take you? Teks are pretty common these days. Were you just convenient or something?"

The first night Dai had been coherent, Terran had explained the whole splice thing to the mercenary. His deepest, darkest secret spilled out easier the second time, and Dai reacted with about as much disgust as Tam. Which was to say, none at all.

It was really, really nice to be around people who didn't think he was some kind of freak. He wasn't used to it. It just made him fall a little bit more in love with his men and made him that much more determined to get them all together.

The silence stretched on, grating on Terran's nerves. He flopped over again, sprawling sideways on the bed. He hung his head over the edge, looking at Dai from upside down. He loved the way it felt, having the blood rushing into his head. All heavy and shit. Very cool.

"Gonna answer me?" he asked.

Dai shot him another look that was probably meant to be irritated but came across as more amused. Terran had found that people had trouble being mad at you when you were upside down. Go figure.

"We're a lot more…integrated than most Teks," Dai finally replied.

"Integrated?"

"Most Teks are really just enhanced humans. They've had implants added as adults, technological body modifications mostly. We're altered at a biological level. Grown in a lab, injected with shit growing up."

Terran wrinkled his nose. "That sounds majorly sucktastic."

"Pretty much. Quite frankly, I'm not certain why those bastards singled me out. The scientists made some big goofs with Tam and me. Regular Teks are a lot more effective."

"Goofs?"

"They gave me the logistics and processing enhancements. Tam got the musculature and physical enhancements."

"Whoops," Terran said dryly. Yeah, *that* made a lot of sense. Dai's personality completely followed the leap-without-looking philosophy, while Tam tended to think himself into a corner.

"Although I suppose I made easy prey, wandering alone like I've been. Most Teks work in pairs or teams," Dai thought to add.

"Tam has been equally alone," Terran felt obliged to point out.

"I don't know that."

"Sure you do."

Dai sighed and pinched the bridge of his nose. "Maybe I do. But Tam didn't shut his systems off for ten years. I did. Guess they thought it made me vulnerable. Doesn't matter now."

"Sure it does. They wanted you for something. You and me."

Terran wasn't an idiot. He had a pretty good idea what that something was, but he wanted Dai to say it out loud.

"You'd think after this many centuries humans would give up on the whole super-soldier idea."

"Guess they can't resist." Terran tried to shrug and nearly landed on his head. *Okay, time to come up.* He was getting nauseous.

He sat up, watching the world whirl around him. "So you and Tam are like a one-of-a-kind pair," he mused.

"Hardly a pair."

*Ooooh.* He was going to completely lose his temper pretty soon and just start smacking both his guys around until they saw things his way.

Smacking around… *Brilliant idea alert!*

Terran hopped off the bed. "I'm gonna go check on Tam. See if he needs any help on piloting this baby."

"Don't fly us into another meteor field," Dai called after him in warning. "That last one made me seasick."

"You can't get seasick in a space ship."

"Wanna bet?"

Terran slapped the door closed on Dai in mid-mumble. *Honestly.* One little joyride through space and they acted like he was some kind of menace. He hadn't even scratched the paint job.

Well, maybe just a few scratches. But that ginormous dent in the hull had already been there. Honest.

* * * *

The door swung open with a near-silent hiss. Daior didn't even try to suppress his groan.

"Baby, don't you have something better to do than nag me?"

"Sorry," came that low, familiar voice that always hit him right in the gut. "Didn't know you were in here. Terran said there was some kind of glitch in the environment regulator. I'll just—"

"The what?" Dai asked with confusion. "I've been here for hours. The regulator's just fine."

"Then why—"

The small snick of the door answered his unfinished question. They both turned to stare before lunging.

Tam got there first. He slammed his hand against the panel, muttering curses.

"Terran!" Dai bellowed.

A small giggle floated through the steel plate.

"I swear by all the stars, I'm going to turn that little arse cherry red!"

"I'll help," Tam said. He kept smacking the lock mechanism but the door remained firmly sealed.

"You just had to put in the good stuff, didn't you?" Dai said. Most locking panels were fragile. A good whack from a super-powered fist and they shattered. This one, of course, was made of the expensive glass. The kind that took an explosion before it would even crack.

Dai stalked across the room and punched into the computer access. The panel slid open in the wall to reveal a small screen, keyboard popping out. He tapped a few commands, trying to override the lock.

"Kid's too damn smart for his own good," he snarled in frustration.

Another giggle floated into the room over the main intercom system.

"That's right," a cheerful voice sang. "I'm much smarter. And cuter. So you should just give in. 'Cause I'm not gonna open the door until you two make up."

"Stubborn little puss, isn't he?" Tam's lips twitched.

"Yep!" Terran said over the intercom. "So go make nice!"

"Your arse, my hand," Dai yelled at the ceiling.

"I don't think that's the right incentive to make him behave," Tam said dryly. "He'd probably enjoy it."

They both waited for another smart-ass comment. It didn't come.

"You're the smart one," Dai burst out. "Figure out how to get the blasted door open."

"Why me? You're the one with the brain enhancements."

"Which I haven't used in a fucking decade!"

Dai snapped his mouth shut and took a deep breath when he realised they were practically screaming at each other. Hell, another few minutes and they'd probably be throwing punches and breaking bones. *Just like old times.*

"What exactly does Terran think he's going to accomplish with this little stunt?" Tam asked.

Thinking back over their earlier conversations, it wasn't all that hard to guess. "He's got some crackpot idea about the three of us making a go of something. Wants us to make up. Personally, I think he's just a horny tomcat."

"There's no need to be so insulting," Tam said.

Dai looked at Tam. "Fucking bastard," he said with exaggerated care.

Tam mumbled something and turned his back on Dai.

"What was that?"

Tam whirled back around. "I said you haven't changed at all. You're still the biggest jerk in the universe."

"At least I'm good at something."

Tam's fist clenched at his side, his jaw doing that ticking thing that indicated he was starting to lose his control. Dai felt a perverse sense of satisfaction at still being able to stir up Tam so easily. He braced himself for the first punch, some part of him actually anticipating the fight to come.

Then Tam's muscles eased and he shook his head, anger seeming to slide away. The lines in his craggy face deepened, and weariness etched heavily on his bulky frame. Dai blinked a few times, not quite sure what to do now.

"I may not have changed," Dai said, some of his own anger fading. "But you have. Was a time we would have been slugging it out already."

Tam dropped onto the bed, studying the floor between his booted feet. "It doesn't seem worth the trouble anymore. Not like it ever solved anything. Not between us, anyway."

Dai scrubbed his face with both hands, not quite sure what to do now. The old Tam he knew how to handle. This new Tam seemed more…vulnerable or something. And despite what he might say to the contrary, Dai still cared. Hard not to. This man had been his friend and constant companion since childhood. They'd seen a lot together, done a lot. Relationship aside, Tam was still his oldest and closest friend. He just couldn't bring himself to kick the man when Tam already seemed down and out.

Dai took a seat next to him. They both stared blankly at the floor for long minutes, the silence stretching awkwardly between them.

"I'll drop you off at the nearest spaceport." Tam was the first one to break the stalemate.

"I thought you said it wasn't the safest course to take."

"It's not. I still think you're better off galaxy hopping until we can figure out who these bastards are and how to get them off your back. But this isn't what you want, stuck with me. And I'm coming between you and Terran. You're good together. I think maybe I should just back out."

*Well, hell.* What did Dai say to that? The jerky part of him wanted to agree, take Terran and split. But he knew that wasn't what Terran wanted. And to be honest, was it really what he wanted?

He didn't know anymore. He was a jumbled up mess. Why couldn't this have waited a week or so? His body was still all screwed up, his mind off-kilter. The implants and chips in his brain and body were at war with his human parts, trying to regulate his system and find a balance that hadn't been achieved in far too long. Some days, he didn't know which end was up. And here were the only two men he'd ever loved, asking him to make difficult, life-changing decisions. He just knew he was going to screw it all up. Irreparably. And then he'd end up with neither of them, when what he really wanted was—well, he really wanted both of them.

So why not? Was what Terran asking really so impossible? He and Tam alone didn't work so well. They were too stubborn, too similar. But with someone between them, someone playing referee, someone they both loved…

The problem was if they tried it and it blew up in their faces, then there'd be three heartbroken idiots roaming the galaxy. And Dai would be alone again. He was so sick of being alone.

*Shit.* Since when had he turned into a coward?

Dai came to a sudden decision. He'd probably regret it pretty quickly, but hell, despite his best efforts, his shell wasn't completely impervious. He couldn't resist the temptation any more, not with it sitting right there looking like home.

He turned and tackled Tamesis, taking the man down onto the bed. He wrapped his hands around the larger man's wrists, lodging his knee between Tam's thighs.

Tam struggled briefly, half-heartedly.

"What are you doing?" he protested weakly. At the same time, Tam arched up a bit.

That put more pressure on the sizeable bulge in Daior's pants. There was an answering hardness on Tam's end.

"What does it look like?" Dai asked, staring down into those familiar eyes. Damn, but this felt good. Right. He hadn't realised how much he'd missed the feeling of Tam's body pressed against his until this minute.

"I know what it looks like," Tam replied. "But don't do this if you don't mean it. Please."

That uncharacteristic note of pleading in Tam's voice shook Dai's legendary composure for a second. Damn, had the man really been hurting that much? The thought made his gut twist.

"I can't promise this is going to work," Dai said with complete and, if Tam's wince was any indicator, unwelcome honesty. "But I'm willing to give it a try. As much as it pains me to admit it, I missed you, too, you big idiot."

"Yes, I can tell," Tam said dryly, wriggling a bit more.

Dai groaned as his penis rubbed against Tam's hard stomach. Naked. He wanted to be naked. Right now.

"What about Terran?" Tam protested when Dai moved in for another kiss.

"What about him? This was all his bloody idea."

"But—"

"Stop thinking so much," Dai whispered. He caught the next protest with his lips, driving his tongue deep into Tam's heat. He caressed the ridged skin, rubbing against the roof of Tam's mouth, duelled briefly with the other man's tongue before seeking out the chipped molar. Kissing Tam was so familiar, felt so right.

Felt like where he was supposed to be.

A small body landed on top of Dai. He absorbed the weight with a small grunt and broke the kiss that Tam was starting to return with enthusiasm.

Dai shifted and looked up into a pair of sparkling blue eyes. "Proud of yourself, aren't you?" he asked, trying to sound gruff and annoyed. Judging by the brilliant smile he received, it didn't work.

Terran leaned over and brushed their lips together. Then he arched over Dai's shoulder to drop a kiss on Tam's mouth.

"You didn't really think I'd let you have all the fun without me?" Terran asked.

# Chapter Fourteen

*Oh, yeah.* Terran was proud of himself. And rightly so, if you asked him.

"Brat." Dai's lips quirked with affection as he reached down to cup Terran's arse.

Then Dai's smile turned a bit wicked, and Terran started to rethink the advisability of his grand scheme.

"And I think I still owe someone a spanking."

Dai moved fast, and before Terran could do more than squeak out a protest, he was facedown over Dai's lap, pants around his knees. He squirmed and wriggled. Dai just planted a hand on the small of Terran's back, keeping him in place.

"Tam!" Terran yelled. "Do something!"

Tam chuckled. "You're on your own this time, Little Bit. I happen to agree with Dai. No locking the captain up. It's a big no-no."

"I'm not twelve!"

"You've sure been acting like it." Dai let his hand fly.

Terran squealed at the sting and burn. *Oh, oh that was…really amazing, actually.*

"Daior!"

His protest was token now, each smack of Dai's big palm sending Terran's arousal spiralling a bit higher. The blows kept coming and Terran kept squirming, but his movements changed. Terran couldn't hold back his low groan as he began to hump Dai's knee, rising to meet the spanks that were, as promised, probably turning his arse a pretty shade of red. His skin was flaming, burning and oh, Gods, why hadn't he tried this sooner?

"Damn, that's nice," Tam whispered.

It sent another spike of heat through Terran, this time lodging in his balls. So Terran not only had a heretofore undiscovered kinky streak, he was apparently voyeuristic now, too. As long as it was Tam doing the watching, Terran wasn't really going to complain.

Dai paused in his rapid rhythm on Terran's arse to caress the skin. Another hand joined the motion, sliding down the curve of his spine and dipping into his crease. A bigger hand, not as hot but more calloused.

*Oh. Oh, stars above.* Having both his men touch him, even with such feather light strokes, was better than he had ever imagined. Terran panted, balls tightening until they hurt. He rocked back and forth, trying to get the necessary friction. He nearly screamed in frustration when Dai shifted Terran, leaving him hanging, both literally and physically.

Tam added a hard smack of his own before moving his hand away. Dai immediately took up his abandoned cadence. Terran squirmed and gasped, moaned and pleaded.

"Oh, oh, Gods, more, harder," he begged, his voice barely audible over the loud slap of flesh meeting flesh.

As Terran got closer to the edge, Dai's hand gentled, the blows landing with less and less force until all Terran could focus on was the climax hovering just beyond his reach.

*No, no, not yet.*

"Wait!" he yelled.

Something in his voice must have caught Dai's attention, because Dai stopped his punishing hand.

"I want someone in me," Terran demanded, trying to wriggle off Dai's lap. He froze, struggling to keep from climaxing as his cock brushed Dai's leg.

"Who do you want?" Tam asked.

Terran was shaking, sweat dripping off him. "Don't care," he said. "Just want us all naked. Together. Now."

"I don't know, Dai," Tam murmured. "Do you think he's learnt his lesson?"

"I've learnt, I've learnt," Terran shrieked. "Now do something!"

A smile sounded in Dai's voice. "Well, if he hasn't, we can always try this again."

"True."

*Yes.* Oh, hell, yes, they were revisiting this. But not right now. Right now, he needed to get fucked.

As if hearing his mental plea, one of them flipped Terran over. He landed on the bed, somehow losing his clothes in the process. He groaned when his flaming arse rubbed against the covers. It just made his arousal flare that much higher.

Terran pried open his eyes to view the glorious sight of his two hulking lovers. They were shedding their clothes with rapid efficiency, displaying bulging muscle and gleaming skin. They were perfection, every one of Terran's fevered imaginings come to life. Like a perfectly matched pair of opposites, one dark and one light. Terran had to check his mouth for drool at the sight of the colourful swirls decorating Tam's arms and wrapping around his upper chest. When Tam turned a bit, Terran saw to his utter delight that the tattoos extended along the sculpted muscles of his upper back. Blues and reds, gorgeous tribal markings that he wanted to trace with his tongue. Gleaming blond hair hung to the top of his arse, confined tightly by a strip of leather. It called to him just as strongly as Daior's messy thatch of dark brown hair. Daior stood with hands on his hips, a bit smaller, a bit leaner, but hard and compact. Tam was tall and broad and big. Everywhere. Terran zeroed in on his favourite parts, licking his lips. Daior was longer and thinner, red cock curving up to his stomach and leaking heavily. Tam wasn't nearly as long, but oh, joy. He really, really wanted that inside him.

Terran's hand drifted down his stomach, unconsciously stroking himself. Tam smirked and smacked his hand away, climbing onto the bed like a tiger stalking its prey.

"No touching," Tam chided. "That's ours."

*Ours. Oh, yeah.* He could live with that.

"Yours," Terran agreed. "But you better do something with it soon, or it might fall off."

"Contrary to popular opinion, you can't die of blue balls," Tam teased.

"The hell you can't," Terran said in something suspiciously close to a whimper. "Another few minutes and I'll prove it!"

"Well, we wouldn't want that, now, would we?" Dai said. He dropped down on the bed, making the mattress dip and jump. He threw one arm around Tam's waist and yanked, pulling them down into a giant pile.

Terran gasped. "Can't breathe," he protested.

Weight shifted, and he was now bracketed by his lovers, one on each side, while they roamed their hands freely over him. Terran arched into the touches and let himself go, let himself feel. He didn't worry about actively participating. He couldn't. They'd melted his brain. All gone. Just a large bundle of sensation.

They trailed kisses and touches over his skin, stroking and petting. Everywhere. Everywhere, that is, but where he most wanted it. Terran was only able to relish the touches for a few minutes before his throbbing cock demanded attention.

"Can't," he gasped. "Need more. Please, Dai. Tam, oh Gods. More! Please!"

"How can we resist such a pretty plea?" Tam asked Dai.

"I don't think we can," Daior replied.

In concert, the two dived for his lower body. Terran nearly exploded when hot, moist heat engulfed his cock and balls. He screamed, body strung tight. Sparks flashed behind his eyes. He struggled to open them, wanting to watch, but his eyelids wouldn't cooperate. One of the men used his tongue to tease Terran's slit, the other laved his balls, and Terran couldn't hold back anymore.

His climax exploded out of him with so much force it hurt, shudders racking his body as the pleasure blended into pain and back again.

When the convulsions stopped, Terran was sticky and breathless, limp and exhausted. Two very smug faces grinned at him.

When Terran remembered how to work his lungs, he mumbled, "Wanted someone in me."

"Oh, we're getting to that," Daior assured him with a wicked grin.

*Oh, hell.* They were going to kill him. But what a way to go.

Tam leaned over to take a kiss, humming softly as he tasted Terran. He let himself go, let himself enjoy the sensation. This time, without the guilt. Solid heat pressed into his side, Daior joining the kiss. Almost lazily, they traded caresses and tongues in a three-way meshing of lips and hands that Tam didn't ever want to stop.

Daior growled and nipped at Tam's lower lip. "Need more," he demanded.

Tam hummed again. "Whatever you want, lover," he whispered, losing himself in those dark eyes.

Terran whimpered, and Tam turned his attention to the debauched man sprawling beneath them. Oh, no, he hadn't forgotten about his Little Bit. Not at all.

"I think someone wanted to get fucked," he teased gently.

Terran waved a hand, wrinkling his nose like the prissiest of nobles. "You've worn me out," he declared loftily. "You'll have to wait until later."

Daior chuckled, low and deep and just a little bit wicked. "Oh, baby, who says you need to be active for this?"

Tam licked his lips. "You or me?" he asked, not really caring a whole lot either way.

"You, I think," Dai murmured against the skin of Tam's neck. He nuzzled and nipped before settling in to suck up a nice, dark mark.

Tam groaned and leaned into the sensation, loving the thought of wearing Dai's marks again. "You can "

Dai pulled away with a soft sound, studying his mark with satisfaction. "No, this way I can be in you."

Tam almost lost his control right then and there.

Terran smirked and wiggled his eyebrows. "A Tam sandwich!" he said before dissolving into helpless laughter.

"Oh, you." Tam pounced, digging for the ticklish spots on Terran's lithe body. "That was awful. Just for that, we should make it open-faced."

"You wouldn't dare," Terran squealed around breathless giggles.

"Nah, don't suppose I would." Tam wanted him too much.

"Where's the stuff?" Daior growled, patience clearly running low.

"How should I know? It's your room."

"And it's your ship."

"Good grief," Terran exclaimed. "No wonder you two need me."

"That we do," Tam murmured, leaning down for another kiss.

"Hey, I think it's my turn." Dai moved in, joining Tam in placing heated kisses on their baby.

They pulled back at the same time and Tam started laughing again. Terran was splayed beneath them, arms flung wide and eyes closed, lips pursed in anticipation. When nothing happened for several seconds, he popped open one eyelid.

"More kisses," he ordered.

Tam chuckled again. Damn, he couldn't remember ever laughing this much during sex before.

Daior landed on Tam's back again, sliding his strong arms around to caress Tam's stomach before moving lower. He closed one large, calloused hand around Tam's dick. Tam groaned, hips thrusting, laughter forgotten in a rush of lust.

Terran propped himself on one elbow and licked his lips, his heated gaze fastened on the sight of Daior stroking Tam with steady motions. Terran thickened and hardened, pressed beneath Tam.

"Damn, Dai," Tam whispered in a hoarse voice. "Our baby's ready to go again."

"Good," came the growled reply. "Because I'm not done with either one of you."

Tam sincerely hoped not.

Dai slid his slick fingers along Tam's lower back and rubbed around his anus before pressing in with one finger. Tam started to pant at the feeling, familiar and yet foreign at the same time.

Daior thrust in a second finger, and Tam grunted. "Easy, babe, it's been a while."

"Good."

Dai stroked deeper, loosening muscles and ramping up Tam's arousal. Heat rushed to Tam's face and he knew it wouldn't take long.

"Forget easy," he said. "Hurry up, babe, or I won't last."

A tube of lube came flying over Tam's shoulder, and he quickly squirted some onto his hand. He let it sit a few seconds, warming the gel.

"Scoot over here," he told Terran.

Terran slid up on the pillows and Tam eased down so his lower body was cradled in the space between Terran's legs. Dai kept stroking and probing. Tam's hands were shaking a bit as he slid his own lubed finger into Terran's arse.

Terran started to pant. "Hurry," he urged.

"Trying, babe," Tam replied around a moan. Dai picked that moment to find his gland, and Tam nearly shot then and there.

"Hold up, Dai," he said. "Let me get—"

He cut off when Terran squeezed down around the three fingers now in his small hole.

They were gonna kill him.

"I can't wait any longer," Daior said.

Tam nodded. "Go ahead."

Daior nipped Tam's shoulder, pushing against Tam's sphincter with something a hell of a lot bigger than a finger. Or even two.

Tam held his breath, muscles tensing involuntarily. It had been a really long time. As Daior slowly pushed in, the pressure built, edging past uncomfortable. Tam reached around and grabbed Dai's hip in a tight, desperate grip.

"Give me a sec," he demanded. His arousal had faded a bit under the intense bite of pain. He was kind of glad. At least he had a chance of making it inside the small body under him.

Terran stroked Tam's chest with gentle hands as Tam tried to breathe through the burn. The light touch was enough to alleviate some of the tension. Tam relaxed a bit, and Daior slid the rest of the way in.

Tam's arousal quickly built to a fever pitch again with his lover pressed so deeply inside him. He quickly slicked up his cock, the touch of his own hand on hot flesh threatening to derail his control.

"Ready?" he asked.

"Past ready," Terran assured him.

Tam braced himself and surged in with one long push. Terran keened his pleasure, limber legs wrapping around Tam's waist. Daior tugged until Terran's calves were caught between Dai's front and Tam's back, effectively pinning them all together.

Dai rocked forward then back out. Each thrust jarred Tam, sending him plunging into Terran. They built a swift rhythm to the accompaniment of pleasure-filled moans.

Tam was sweating hard. He wasn't sure which feeling he liked better—Terran wrapped around his cock in a tight vice or Daior ploughing into him with jarring force. Luckily, he didn't have to choose.

"Tam!"

Terran gasped his name, body arching and muscles contracting around Tam's cock as he shot, covering Tam's chest in sticky heat.

Daior growled into Tam's ear. "He's so gorgeous when he loses it."

Daior's words and the thick cock brushing his prostate were all Tam needed. He shouted, filling Terran's arse. Dai wasn't far behind. A few more powerful strokes, and Tam's own arse was flooded. He collapsed onto Terran, arms giving out.

Terran gasped. "Guys! Can't breathe!"

With a grumble, Daior rolled aside. They cuddled together, Tam still scrunched in the middle.

And loving it.

Daior flopped his arm over Tam's waist and pulled him onto his side and into that broad chest. Dai wrapped his hand around Terran's hip, tugging him in closer. Tam flung a leg over Terran's. The small man snuggled in with a sigh of contentment.

"Could stay like this all day," Terran mumbled sleepily.

"Go for it," Tam replied. Heck, he didn't think he'd move for a couple of days. He was exhausted, physically and emotionally.

Dai's presence was a heavy weight at his back, Terran a comforting touch at his front. Tam savoured the close contact. After nearly ten years alone, he was in heaven.

Sleep hovered at the corner of his mind, He tried to embrace it fully, but doubts were starting to creep in. Now that the sex was over, would they still want him around? Was there a place for him with the two men he…hell, the two men he loved?

Tam wasn't afraid to admit it to himself, although he damn sure wasn't ready to admit it to them.

"Stop worrying so much," Daior said.

The man still knew him far too well.

"I'm not." The protest wasn't really believable, but Tam felt he had to at least make an effort.

"Would you two shut up?" Terran ordered. "Trying to sleep here."

Tam chuckled and finally succeeded in pushing the doubts away for later. For now, he was just going to enjoy holding his men.

After all, Terran had demanded it. And for all his size, Tam wasn't under any illusions. The two big, hardened mercenaries were not the ones in control in this relationship.

For some reason, he couldn't feel too bothered by it.

Tam slipped into sleep, content for the first time in a very, very long while.

# Chapter Fifteen

Terran was itchy again. Marvin was something of a miracle worker, and the concoction of various medications and vitamins he'd mixed up to keep the weirdness at bay was working. Sort of. But Terran's body kept spiking and...well, his brain wouldn't shut up. Questions kept rolling around in his mind, and the stupid, not-quite-human part of him wouldn't give up until he got them answered. Daior was being grumpy again, go figure. You'd think all the hot, sweaty sex would put him in a better mood. But Terran had tried talking to Daior twice today and just got irritated grunts from his lover. And a really scorching kiss, which had made his day a lot better. But it didn't help with the itches.

So Terran went looking for Tamesis.

Tam might be the quieter of the two men, but he was still the one most likely to answer Terran's questions. More likely to share. Dai would growl and grump then kiss Terran some more until Terran forgot his own name, let alone whatever it was he'd wanted to ask.

Tam held court on the bridge, settled back in the captain's chair and studying the data screens. Terran plopped onto his lap and wrapped his arms around the large man's neck. He nuzzled in happily. Tam had the perfect lap for cuddling.

"Hey there," came the raspy welcome. Tam tugged him close. "Where's Daior?"

"Doing some weird sword thing in the exercise room."

"His systems aren't regulating correctly just yet," Tamesis gently admonished Terran's implied complaint.

"I still don't understand all that."

Tamesis shrugged. "It's complicated. Simple version? The tech in his body was off too long. It's trying to readjust to working in tandem with Dai's biological systems."

"I still don't get it," Terran declared. "But that wasn't why I came looking for you."

"Oh?"

Oooh, that glint in Tam's eyes was pure evil. Terran loved it. He giggled. "Not that. No, I had a question."

"Hmmm?"

"What happened between you two?"

The tension that invaded Tam's muscles was slight, but Terran still felt it.

Tam shrugged, trying for a nonchalance he clearly didn't feel. "We just proved…non-compatible."

"Bullshit," Terran declared succinctly.

Tamesis growled.

Terran scowled. Tam met his scowl with stubborn silence. All right, so Terran would need to apply more pressure. Before he could act, though, Tam sighed.

"We're too much alike," Tam said.

"I don't think you're anything alike," Terran protested.

"When it comes to being lovers, we are."

"What, you both like to top?"

Tam snorted on his laugh. "Sex was never the problem with us. It was everything else we screwed up."

Tamesis shook his head. Terran was wearing that damned mulish look on his cute features again.

"Come on," Terran wheedled. "What was so bad that Dai cut you off for ten years?"

"It wasn't just me he cut off. It was an entire part of himself, too."

"Why?"

"Our last job together…didn't go well."

And that was probably the biggest understatement Tam had ever uttered. Damn, but he had been a complete idiot.

"What happened?"

"You never give up, do you?"

"Nope."

"Ask Dai."

"I'm asking you."

"Well, ask him."

"He won't tell me."

Tamesis sighed in exasperation, although he wasn't really all that irritated. If they were going to make this thing work, Terran would need to know, eventually.

"You're going to keep bugging me until I give in, aren't you?"

That bright head nodded emphatically. "Yep. I'll follow you around the ship like a shadow. And talk. Incessantly"

Tam laughed. "What are we going to do with you, Little Bit?"

"Cuddle me. Tell me all your secrets. Make wild, passionate, monkey sex."

Tam laughed again, hard enough to drive the air from his lungs. "What the hell does that even mean?"

Terran shrugged. "I don't know. It sounds awesome and dirty, though, doesn't it?"

Tam's little lap-mate bounced a bit. Tam grunted as that tight arse bumped some vital bits. He grabbed Terran around the hips to anchor him in place.

"Gonna tell me now?"

"If I do, will you kiss me?" Tam teased, knowing full well he would spill every single one of his deepest, darkest secrets to this man without any incentive at all. Probably before the week was out.

"Oh, I can do better than that," Terran said.

Tam didn't trust that grin, not one bit. "How much better?"

"Blowjob?"

The thought of those luscious lips wrapped around his cock had him hardening so fast the blood loss made him dizzy.

"Fuck," he gasped.

"After the blowjob," Terran assured him. "But not until you talk."

"Damn, you would make one hell of an interrogator."

Terran grinned, and damn if that that smile didn't just light up the whole room. "Only for you. And Dai," he added.

"Damn right," Tam grunted. The thought of his Terran in anyone's arms but his or Dai's made him want to rip something apart. Preferably whoever dared to touch what was his. Theirs. That might take some getting used to. But he loved it. Him, Daior and Terran. As close to heaven as someone like him was probably ever going to get.

He was okay with that.

Tamesis looked down into expectant blue eyes and sighed again. While Terran had a true gift for bouncing from one thought to another, he could be irritatingly single-minded when he chose to be.

"We took a job guarding a mine a few solar systems over. Really rough territory, no true settlement. Just four huge mines, a couple of brothels and saloons. That was about it. We were hired by one of the owners. He'd been having some problems. Thefts, sabotage, the usual crap. Two of the mines were owned by the same man, Carter, and he had his eye on acquisition. We'd been working the job about two weeks when things came to a head. Full-out war. It was a hell of a mess. One of the independent mines got blown to scraps. The next thing we knew, a couple of hundred armed miners were going at it. The two independent owners decided to cut their losses. They asked Dai and me to conduct the negotiations. They didn't trust Carter any farther than they could throw him, and they were both big guys."

He paused, mind skipping over the past. That planet had been the biggest hellhole he'd ever worked. Actually, the whole thing had been one giant clusterfuck. They should never have taken the job in the first place. Hindsight and all that. But then, if it hadn't been the Carter mess, it would have been something else. The break had been a long time coming.

Tamesis took a deep breath before continuing. "Dai had been injured on our last mission. Nothing major, a bullet to the shoulder, but it kind of freaked me out. Maybe, if he hadn't still been sporting a bandage, I wouldn't have done it. But chances were really good that whoever walked into those negotiations wasn't walking out in one piece."

Terran suddenly sat up straighter. "Wait a minute. Carter. Mine owner. Entrepreneur. Erasmus Carter, Lord Protector of Marquos?"

"Yeah, that would be the bastard."

Terran winced. Tam knew what he was thinking. Anyone who roamed the galaxies had heard of Carter. It was hard to avoid him. 'Bastard' was an accurate—and generous—description for the man. Carter was known for his hard-ass attitude. When he wanted something, he got it. You either got out of his way or you died. There was no middle ground with the guy. He wasn't kind and he was very rarely merciful. You counted yourself fortunate if you crossed him and got a quick death. Carter's preferred methods were slow and painful.

"You did something stupid, didn't you?" The sentence came out more like a statement than a question.

Tam gave the small man a warning squeeze. "You want to hear this or not?"

Terran snapped his mouth shut again.

"Stupid would be one way of putting it, yes," Tam admitted. "I decided to do the noble thing. As if I know the first thing about being noble." Tam added the last with a little derisive snort.

Terran looked like he wanted to protest again, but Tam rode right over it.

"I decided to leave Daior out of the meeting. So, I locked him on our ship."

"Oh, Tam."

"Yeah. Not one of my brighter moments. I made it out of the meeting with Carter intact, but I wasn't quite so lucky with Dai. Seems he didn't appreciate my attempt to protect him. Idiot broke my nose and my arm and tried his damnedest to break my neck, too. Thought he was going to finish off the job Carter started. After that, he dropped out of sight. Swore he'd never speak to me again, de-activated his systems and took off. I didn't see him or even catch a hint of a rumour about him until he called me in to get you off that planet. And I think he probably would have let himself die there if it weren't for you."

"Oh, I'm sure not," Terran protested.

Tam shook his head and smiled but knew it was a sad expression, at least if it were projecting any of his feelings. He still felt it, in the pit of his stomach, dull and resigned. "No, Bit. I know Dai, probably better than he knows himself sometimes. He would have clung to that stubborn insistence even if it killed him. But he wasn't going to risk your life."

"I really don't think I'm that important to him."

Tamesis looked incredulously at the small man on his lap. "Are you joking? Have you not seen the way Daior looks at you? He'd cut out his own heart if you asked him to."

"Ewww." Terran wrinkled his nose. "But he cares about you, I can see it."

"Sometimes that isn't enough. Me cutting him out like that, it pushed him over the edge. When I care about someone, I sometimes have trouble restraining myself from…coddling them. Dai doesn't take too well to coddling."

"No kidding," Terran drawled. "What about Dai?"

"What about him?"

"Well, if you were too protective, what was he?"

"Grumpy."

"Tam!"

"No, I'm serious. I tend to over think everything, take life seriously. Dai needed someone willing to play every once in a while. I couldn't give that to him."

"So, you need someone to protect. Dai needs someone to laugh at him."

"Something like that."

"Did it ever occur to you," Terran asked, "that I just might be the gooey centre you need?"

"That's what I'm counting on."

Terran snuggled into Tam's chest, a satisfied sigh coming from him. Tam wanted to echo it. For the first time in remembered history, he was completely and utterly satisfied with his life at this particular moment in time. So they had a bunch of nutcase scientists on their back. So they were on the run from more than a few people who would like to dissect them into small pieces and put them back together in weird configurations.

He had his men. Life was pretty darn perfect from where he sat.

# Chapter Sixteen

Terran poked at the gelatinous liquid with one finger, eyeing it with suspicion.

"What is it?" he asked the merchant.

"A new fuel source," the man proudly told him.

"Huh," Terran said. "Looks like it would gunk up the engines in ten minutes."

"Oh no, no. It is clean. Very clean."

"It looks…goopy. And covered in mould."

The man stared at him blankly.

Terran rolled his eyes. "Goopy. Sticky and nasty and…oh, never mind."

The man's broad face crinkled in irritation.

"Terran!" Dai's voice.

Terran sighed at the yell and turned. "What now?" he asked of no one in particular.

Daior came bustling through the crowd, eyes constantly moving, face set in a dark scowl. It didn't escape Terran's notice that the shopkeeper backed into the shadows of his little stall.

They had stopped to pick up supplies on a teeny, tiny planet in the same system as the Indara Spaceport. In fact, the merchant district in the town bore more than a passing resemblance to the one on Indara. Except with dust. A lot of dust.

Dai slid to a stop, literally, his feet having trouble finding purchase on the thick layer of dirt coating the street, which was paved with an uneven combination of brick and stone.

"I told you three times to stay close," Dai scolded. "And what do you do? Disappear. I blink and you're gone."

Terran shrugged. It wasn't his fault he tended to get distracted by shiny things. And the lure of the hawkers was just so dang hard to resist sometimes.

"Did you find him?" Tam pushed through the crowd next, broad shoulders easily clearing a path. Hell, anyone with sense would get out of the man's way. He stood nearly a head taller than...well, just about everyone.

"Yes," Terran said around an exasperated sigh. "He found me. I was looking at this...gunk. It's supposed to fuel a ship, but I think—"

"Terran!"

"That's my name and you're wearing it out."

Dai's scowl deepened. "Someone is practically begging to go back over my knee."

"I don't—"

"That's enough out of both of you," Tam interrupted.

Terran sighed. His foot tapped a rapid tattoo on the street, jitters making him twitchy. He felt uneasy, off-balance, like his skin didn't fit. It wasn't the usual itchiness he associated with his non-human DNA rearing its head, either. No, this was something else entirely. It had started as soon as they'd landed on-planet and had grown worse every minute. Gelatinous goo, no matter how fascinating, could only distract him for so long.

"Terran, what has got into you?" Tam pressed. "You're feisty, but you're not usually this bratty."

"I just feel like—Ooh, pretty."

Dai sighed. "And he's off again."

"I just hope to the Gods it's not another parrot."

"What?"

"Nothing. Be glad you missed it. In hindsight, it was rather disturbing. Amusing, but disturbing."

Terran stroked his hand over the bright red fabric of a hand-woven blanket, swallowing a purr at the slip of soft cloth under his fingertips. Oh, that would be just marvellous to cuddle up under.

"Dai, can I—"

A flash of light caught Terran's attention, and he turned, narrowing his eyes. Despite what his men might think, he wasn't nearly as distracted and flighty as he was behaving. An unpredictable target was harder to catch. And right now, he felt like a target. With a big, red circle painted right on his back.

Terran slipped to the side a bit farther, still pretending absorption in the colourful wares displayed so neatly. Tam was in serious conversation with the merchant, Daior hovering at Terran's side like a big, black cloud.

"I think we should head back to the ship," Dai said.

Terran watched out of the corner of his eye as Tam paid the merchant. The blanket didn't hold as much interest for Terran anymore, though. His attention had been diverted by movement at the edge of the crowd.

"I think you're right," Terran replied quietly. "We're being watched. Three doors down, under the awning."

"Yeah. I don't think he's your average pickpocket, either."

It didn't really surprise Terran that Dai had noticed. What did surprise him was that they hadn't made a run for it yet. Dai was, if nothing else, obsessive about safety. Particularly Terran's safety.

Tam looked over, meeting Daior's eyes. A silent message passed between them. Dai nodded.

Just like that, Tam was gone. And how the heck a big guy like that could vanish so easily, Terran had no idea. He started to follow, but the grip on his arm stopped him.

"Stay here," Dai murmured. "We're the bait."

"Oh."

Bait? That sounded rather ominous. In all the old movies Terran had ever seen, things never ended well for the bait.

Terran tapped his foot, waiting impatiently. Hours seemed to pass, but he was honest enough to admit it was probably only a minute or two. Three, tops.

"Can we—"

"No."

"But I want to—"

"No."

"Tam—"

"No."

Terran opened his mouth.

"No," Dai insisted before Terran could speak.

"You're no fun," Terran pouted.

"I try."

More time passed as the crowd ebbed and flowed through the square, Daior's menacing presence creating a nice little bubble of space around them.

Terran jumped, uttering an embarrassing little squeak, when Tam appeared as suddenly as he had vanished.

"Where did you come from?" Terran demanded with a scowl.

Tam roundly ignored the complaint. "We need to move. He's an advance. There's a little bunch of mercenaries headed our way, and they're armed to the teeth. Here and now isn't the time to start a war."

"Right."

Terran found himself grabbed by each arm and unceremoniously escorted through the streets.

"We could move faster if you'd let go," he pointed out.

Damn it, this was getting ridiculous. Terran wasn't stupid and he wasn't helpless. And the low opinion the two seemed to have of his intelligence *hurt.* He wasn't going to do something reckless. Not when there was actual danger involved.

The hair on the back of Terran's neck prickled. He dug in his feet, earning furious glares. He lifted his head and sniffed the air.

"Not that way," Terran said.

"It's the most—"

"Would you please trust me?" Terran hated the pleading tone in his voice, but he didn't have time for pride. He needed the guys to listen to him and he needed them to do it now. "I know what I'm doing. And we don't want to go that way."

Tam gave in first, nodding and loosening his grip on Terran's arm. It took Dai a little longer to follow suit, but he finally did.

Terran immediately darted into a narrow side street. He could hear Daior cursing as the pair followed him.

His instincts were running high, tension stringing his body tight. He rounded another corner and slid to a halt, muttering a soft curse.

"What is it, Terran?"

Terran looked up at Tam's concerned face. "The scout had friends."

"Yeah, they're on the way."

Terran shook his head. "No, other friends. Already-here friends."

"Damn, I must be losing my touch."

Daior narrowed his eyes at the dim alley ahead of them and shook his head. "There's only three in front. I think our best plan is to barrel through and run for the ship."

"Sounds good," Terran said.

His men turned two pairs of hard eyes, glaring at him.

"You'll stay here," Daior said grimly. "We'll yell when we've cleared a path."

"Oh, no you don't." It was rare that Terran got angry, truly angry, but he was getting there now.

"It's safer that way." Tam added his opinion in a quieter, but no less firm, voice.

"Correct me if I'm wrong, but isn't an attitude like this exactly what broke up the two of you last time? I appreciate you wanting to protect me, and most of the time I'm okay with it. But I'm not letting you go off into danger while I wait behind like a helpless kid. So

I'm going with you, and if you try to argue again, I will bite you. And you won't like it."

Tam snorted, a sound he quickly tried to smother when Daior glared furiously at him.

"Terran, we can't protect you and fight at the same time," Dai pressed with ill-concealed impatience.

"I don't need protecting. Not from this lot."

They were wasting precious time, time they didn't have if they wanted to get out of town before reinforcements hit.

When in doubt, force the issue. It was only one of many mottos by which Terran ruled his life. He might not be big and strong like his guys, but he was sneaky and fast.

He used those traits to his advantage now. He darted to one side and was past Daior and nearly to the end of the alley before the big lug could react.

A roar of fury followed his progress, but Terran kept going. It was time for his men to realise he wasn't completely helpless. And with the two big mercenaries to pull him out if he got in over his head, well, what was there to worry about?

Plenty, as it turned out. Terran just hadn't anticipated how *big* his opponents would be.

The three mercenaries weren't carrying guns, but they didn't need them. Their sheer size alone would be all the deterrent they needed.

Terran had time enough for an 'Oh, shit' moment before they were on him. He dodged between the legs of the giant guy with blue hair, rolled and came up behind him to look right at an even larger man with green skin.

Greenie went down pretty easily when Terran kicked him in the balls, but he bounced right back up like a flower on jacked-up fertiliser. Terran heard bodies thud together behind him, but he didn't take his eyes off the predator in front of him.

Terran licked his lips, flicking his tongue along the sharp edge of his canine teeth.

Time for some strategy.

Terran straightened from his crouched, attack-ready position and smiled, glancing up from under hooded eyes. He even batted his lashes a touch for extra effect.

"What took you so long?" he purred.

Greenie blinked at him with bewildered, red eyes.

Terran struck. Unfortunately, besides being large, the mercenary was much faster than Terran had anticipated. Terran found himself grasping empty air as he whipped by the already moving man.

Terran was good at improvising. He whirled on one foot and launched himself into the air. His angle was true, and he latched onto Greenie's neck, clinging to the mercenary's back like a leech to its prey.

"What the hell?" Greenie twisted and wriggled, but his long arms weren't quite long enough to pry Terran off his back. Terran dug his knees into a bony spine and squeezed with his arms.

Greenie had a neck like an elephant. No matter how hard Terran squeezed, he couldn't seem to restrict air flow enough to knock out his target.

Terran scowled and kicked the man in the bum in irritation.

"Need some help?"

Terran scowled harder, this time the expression aimed over Greenie's head at a smirking Daior.

"No," he snapped. "I'm just going to stay here the rest of the afternoon."

He could, too. But it was kind of like that old Earth saying, the one about having a tiger by the tail. You couldn't lose the fight—or win it, for that matter—but you couldn't retreat, either. Letting go meant getting eaten.

"Stop teasing, Daior," Tam rumbled admonishingly. "We don't have time."

They moved in tandem, Tam plucking Terran off Greenie's back while Daior laid out the man with impressive speed. When all three attackers were lying in unconscious heaps, they started to make their own retreat.

"I have to admit, Little Bit, you did pretty good," Tam said, ushering Terran out of the alley and around yet another corner.

"What do you mean?" Terran resisted the urge to pout. "You had to help me."

"But you didn't get hurt and you kept him distracted for us. In my book, that's a success."

"And I think you need a new book." Daior glowered at them both.

Terran perked up anyway.

In this particular battle, he'd take whatever he could get. Any acknowledgement that maybe Terran wasn't helpless after all would be greeted with happy acceptance.

They made it back to the *Farion* without any further incidents. Tam and Terran ran through the take-off procedures while Daior cleared them with the port officials. Tam took over the controls before Terran could, and they were up and moving away within moments.

With extreme caution, they slipped through the port of hovering ships that were waiting for an open dock.

This was the most dangerous part of any space travel. Not the asteroid belts or the meteor fields or the unexpected debris showers. No, it was the blasted airborne parking lots.

The *Farion* passed a tiny transport ship with only inches to spare, and Terran caught a glimpse of the markings on it.

"Magnify," he ordered the ships controls.

A tiny portion of the viewing screen zoomed in on the small insignia on the ship's tail, and Terran winced.

"Our friends?" Daior asked.

"Worse," Terran said. "My brother."

"Wave hello, baby." Daior took his own advice, waving cheerfully at the other ship. The fact they couldn't see him was, of course, completely beside the point.

Terran groaned and dropped his face into his hands. "Can we just get away from this blasted planet?" Terran pleaded.

"Working on it, Bit."

They finally cleared the lot, and Tam hit the hyperdrive. As they shot towards deep space, another vessel appeared on their radar, close on their tail.

"More visitors," Tam remarked.

"Ten Gods, how many coincidences can we run afoul of in one day?"

Terran patted Dai soothingly. "Want me to drive?"

Two voices shouted a denial. Terran slid down in his chair, crossing his arms and pouting.

"Fine," he said. "But you'd better lose them fast so we can go have some fun."

Tam grinned. "Anything for you."

It only took them half an hour to lose their pursuers. Terran thought with satisfaction that it certainly helped to have the proper motivation.

He'd have to remember that for future situations.

# Chapter Seventeen

The sensors were going crazy. Layna covered her ears while Richard bellowed curses at his beleaguered junior communications officer.

"What the hell is going on?"

"I think… Sir, I think that was the ship we've been tracking."

"So why the hell am I only *now* being alerted?"

"Something was blocking our—"

"Turn this thrice-cursed crate around!" Richard roared, loudly enough so that a couple of his crew winced as their earpieces squealed.

"Umm…"

"Now!"

"Can't, Captain," his pilot stated matter-of-factly. "We're packed in here tighter than a bunch of Crenellians in an isopod."

Richard didn't even pretend to understand what that was supposed to mean. No one ever understood

Fahey's sayings. Richard was privately convinced the man made most of them up.

Richard growled out another curse. That blasted vein in his forehead was throbbing again and he wouldn't be surprised if his eyes were turning red with the force of his rage.

He glared in impotent fury at the retreating cruiser, ready to just throw up his hands and consign his brother to whatever corner of hell would welcome the little brat.

Unfortunately, Richard couldn't do that, no matter how much the thought enticed him. Terran was Richard's responsibility, whether either of them liked it or not.

"Getting ready to dock, Captain," Fahey announced.

Layna shrugged. "Might as well poke around a bit," she commented blandly. "We won't be able to get departure clearance for at least an hour. We'll be lucky to pick up more than a vapour trail by then."

"Shit." Richard narrowed his eyes in thought but finally was forced to concede that Layna was right. They couldn't go tearing off after Terran at present. Best to see what they could find out here. Maybe someone, somewhere, would know something about the owner of that blasted cruiser. Terran had picked up some companions somewhere along the line, and Richard wanted to know who, what, where, when and how. Forewarned was forearmed and all that. Richard was a big believer in being prepared.

Less than half an hour later, Richard stood staring with dumbfounded shock at the carnage in the little alley. A geek patrol member had used one of their little magic gadgets to track Terran's trail. Richard was used to weird happenings around his brother and, he was proud to admit, almost completely inured to the path of destruction Terran usually managed to leave behind.

This, however, was a bit much, even for him. A trio of heavily-muscled, heavily-enhanced Teks lay sprawled in unconscious, bloody glory over the cracked pavement. A pair of security personnel were busy chattering on their radios and trying to keep spectators at a distance.

Taking the initiative, and with that easy, disarming charm that always surprised Richard, Layna sidled up to one of them. She returned after a few minutes of low-voiced conversation.

"Well?" Richard asked.

Layna shook her head and pulled him aside. "I think we should leave these nice men to their job," she said, loudly enough for said men to hear and exchange large, pleased grins.

Richard let Layna drag him a few blocks before the need for answers got the better of him.

"Talk to me, Lieutenant."

"Security doesn't know anything. Said by the time they heard noises, the fight was over."

"So, not evenly matched?"

"Completely *out*-matched," Layna agreed. "Whoever took on these guys, they were pros. Those Teks back there didn't come cheap. They were high-end and high-class all the way. Despite the blue hair, I think at least two of them were Malkaians."

"Damn." Richard rubbed his forehead. Malkaians. What the hell had his brother got into? "So we don't know much more than we did before."

Layna's smile was huge and so smug that it actually made Richard a bit nauseous. A smile like that usually meant one of two things—fun at his expense, or a victory she could gloat over for the next couple of years.

"There was a nice little camera recording a good deal of the scene from the rooftop of the bookstore. Seems they like to hold a little illegal poker game there every week."

"And it caught everything?"

Layna nodded. "Everything."

Richard was about to gnaw off his own arm in frustrated impatience by the time they finally made it back through the crowded port, received take-off clearance and docked back with the *Celsius*.

Luckily, Richard's technical geniuses had worked their magic by that point and hacked into the local police database. Richard returned to the main communications room, a large, bright space next to the bridge that was always humming with people and equipment, to find a video playing on a loop of the day's earlier events.

The geek patrol was gathered around the video, hooting and hollering. Richard had to admit, although certainly not aloud, that the show was impressive. And he was hard-pressed to suppress his smile when his little brother went all monkey on his attacker's back. As much as Terran might frustrate him, Richard did admire his spirit.

Richard just wished there was some caution—and common sense—to go with the spirit.

He stood behind the group of spectators and cleared his throat. Amazing how quickly his crew ducked back to their stations.

He studied the fight, watching the utter effortlessness with which Terran's two companions dispatched their prey.

"What do you think?" he asked Layna.

"I think," Layna said, holding up a piece of paper, "that we have some names."

Richard let his smile slip free, although judging by the wary glances he was getting, the expression was probably as cold as it felt.

"Then let's go bag a couple of Teks," he said.

*Oh, yeah.* With his connections and the names of not only the men but their ship as well, there was no place in the galaxy that could hide the three.

He'd have his brother back before the little brat knew what hit him.

# Chapter Eighteen

Tam tilted back in the large, extremely comfortable captain's chair on the bridge of his little cruiser. He'd installed the chair himself, one of many modifications. He figured if a guy was going to roam around space, he ought to do it in comfort.

He stretched his arms overhead, groaning a bit as tense muscles lengthened. He yawned, his gaze lazily scanning the data screens for any anomalies.

Gods, he was tired. He thought longingly of Terran and Daior, curled up in their bedroom. Where he'd been until that damn sense of responsibility dragged him out from under Terran's fluffy new red blanket. But with their narrow escape of earlier, Tam didn't trust the scanners to keep them safe. Sometimes, it took a human touch.

Tam yawned again, blinking his eyes a few times when his vision went a bit fuzzy. It had been three standard days since Terran had worn them down and wrapped all three of them up in his nice, crazy little relationship. Tam couldn't regret it, even thinking deep down that he'd probably end up with a stomped-on heart.

Although so far, things were working out surprisingly well. Or maybe not so surprisingly. He and Daior had always done well together. They just needed someone to referee between them, someone they could coddle and protect, someone to brighten their world and lighten their spirits.

And Terran? He needed two people just to keep up with him. The little brat had enough energy for four people. Tam wasn't used to having so much sex. His balls were actually sore. A good sore, but sore all the same. It seemed like Terran could close his eyes for five minutes then be up and ready to go. Literally.

Tam chuckled a bit to himself, picturing the contented, sated expression on Terran's face earlier. Yeah, he did like that look.

He tipped his chair back some more, propping his boots up on the console, and tucked his arms behind his head. Involuntarily, his eyes started to slip closed.

A loud crash nearly sent him to the floor. Tam's boots slipped off the console, and he pitched forward, grabbing hold of the long instrument panel that ran around the nose of the ship. A quick glance at the clock showed him he'd been out for nearly two hours.

*Now what?* Tam cursed to himself as he punched up the main viewing screen.

"Damn it to the Seventh Ring," he spat. They'd been found. So much for their little rollercoaster ride through the asteroid belt. The bastards were still on their trail. *Close* on their trail. As in, riding their arse. With a lot of firepower.

The alarms went off—finally—as the bristling warship let loose with another round of low-level blasts. The rapid firing guns were meant to disable, not to destroy. So the jerks wanted them alive, which unfortunately still left far too many suspects. So, Richard or the kidnappers?

The ship dipped from side to side, and Tam shoved the question aside. Didn't really matter right now. Get away first, figure out the details later.

Although he was growing really, really tired of always running.

Tam slid the chair sideways in its track, firing up the engines to maximum power and trying desperately to swing the *Farion* around.

A second alarm joined the first as shudders rocked the cabin. The piercing electronic scream made it hard to think. Tam let loose with another round of curses as he tried to find the right alarm and shut it off while simultaneously diverting more power to the shields and trying to manoeuvre the *Farion* into a better position.

Dai came sliding around the corner wearing nothing but a pair of pants. They were Tam's, riding low on his more slender hips. Dai grabbed the waistband with one hand to keep them up. "Please tell me you have weapons on this gods-damn crate," he bellowed.

"What do you think?" Tam bellowed back.

"Then open 'em up!"

"Bastards are in my blind spot."

Terran staggered through the door next, the force of another blast nearly knocking him off his feet. Despite arriving after Dai, Terran was still stark naked. His bright hair stood on end, eyes taking up more space than usual on his face.

"What?" he asked, voice cracking a bit at the end. "We aren't really under attack, are we?"

"Bet your sweet arse we are," Dai replied succinctly.

"But—"

"Damn it," Tam snarled. "I can't get a clear shot."

Dai stared at the vidscreen with visible disbelief. "She's right in front of you. Broadside. How the hell can you *not* get a clear shot?"

"Cruisers don't exactly come equipped for battle," Tam replied, heavy on the sarcasm. "I had to make the mods myself. The pulse cannons are in one of the storage bays. I need to be parallel, and I don't have the room to manoeuvre."

"Out of the way," Terran ordered briskly.

Tam reluctantly let Terran replace him at the controls, where Terran quickly busied himself resetting switches. Another shudder rocked the *Farion*, the sound of tearing metal echoing throughout the cabin.

"That's not good," Dai announced to no one in particular.

"You might want to hold on to something," Terran said.

Tam was already busy strapping himself tightly in the co-pilot's chair. "I'd take that advice," he said.

Dai looked at the screen, looked at the controls and shook his head. "Uh uh. No way do you make a turn like that. Best to engage hyper drive and try to shoot past them."

"One of those shots took out the hyper drive," Terran said grimly. "The vertical thrusters are toast, too. It'll be a tight fit, but I can manage."

"Baby, I don't think—"

"Dai, shut up and hang on," Tam advised.

"He's that good?"

"That's right, you were asleep the last time. Lucky bastard," Tam added.

"I don't like the sound of that."

"Hang on," Terran shouted.

"Damn, we need another chair," Dai muttered. Then he braced himself in the nearest corner.

Terran slammed the cruiser into forward and threw his weight against the wheel. The engines screamed in protest as the ship tried to shoot ahead. Terran flipped switches with astonishing rapidity, keeping the cruiser in place. Tam's stomach dropped to his feet as the small space vessel seemed almost to jump straight up. Without the vertical thrusters. Shudders rippled through the hull and another screech of metal, this one caused by the internal pressure building up in the engine room, made him wince.

"Pull back," Dai shouted. "You're gonna fry the—"

The engines died with shocking suddenness. Terran had a white-knuckled grip on the steering column and was panting, sweat staining dark the roots of his bright hair. He was visibly shaking. Their little man took a deep breath and forced his hands to let go.

"Take your shot," Terran said in a hoarse voice.

Tam blinked at the vidscreen. "Holy hell and all the little fishes," he whispered. Then he grinned wildly. He pulled up the weapon panel and switched on the guns. The ship jumped and shuddered again, but this time Tam welcomed it. Puffs of smoke appeared on the smooth casing of their attacker's ship. He always found it weird, the way there was such violence on the screen but no sound. Explosions should have sound.

"Holy shit," Dai said, standing to hover over Tam's shoulder. "I didn't think a turn like that was possible."

"Laws of physics say it shouldn't be," Tam replied, sending another barrage at their enemy. He picked off an incoming missile with ease.

"The laws of physics are overrated," Terran said.

All three watched in satisfaction as the image in the vidscreen dissipated in a blinding flash of light.

When the fireworks subsided, they were left staring at a field of wreckage. Twisted metal and scraps of plastic floated in stasis, stretching between them and the nearby bulk of an uninhabited planet.

"Damn," Daior commented. "Where the hell did you get those guns? They sliced through the shields like they weren't even there."

"A little workshop in Myria that deals with the highly dangerous and highly illegal."

"Very nice."

Tam unstrapped himself from the chair before doing the same for Terran. He hauled their lover up and hugged him tightly before passing the nearly limp form on to Dai.

"You did good, baby," Dai murmured, burying his head in Terran's hair.

Terran gave a little whimper and wrapped himself around Dai's body. "I wasn't sure I could do it," he admitted in a tortured voice.

"You're one hell of a pilot, Little Bit," Tam reassured their lover. He reached over to rub Terran's back for a minute before returning his attention to the cruiser's control systems. "Now, we should get out of here before reinforcements arrive."

"I think I might have blown up the engines," Terran admitted.

"Looks like I can reroute enough reserve power to make a short jump," Tam said, reading the results of the ship-wide scan he'd initiated. "Should get us far enough away that we're out of detection range. But it's gonna be rough."

Dai sat in Terran's recently vacated chair and settled their exhausted lover on his lap. "Just get us out of here," Dai ordered.

They exchanged significant looks over Terran's head, both apparently thinking the same thing.

With the engines so badly damaged, they might as well park themselves in the middle of the busiest space port around and paint a giant target on the top of the *Farion*.

Tam sighed and occupied himself with the controls, hoping like hell for a miracle. The *Farion* shook violently, engines revving and dying with a squeal of protest. It took him five tries just to get enough power diverted into the jump drive. The lights flickered then died completely, the drive sucking every scrap of energy. And in the end, they didn't even make it to the next galaxy. The *Farion* dropped out of warp far too close to their starting point for Tam's peace of mind, but his ship just didn't have anything else in her. He sighed, rubbing at his eyes.

"All right," he said to no one in particular. "Let's go see how bad it is."

# Chapter Nineteen

Terran chewed anxiously on his lower lip as he watched Tam flip through the data on the tablet clutched in his hand. Tam kept muttering under his breath and Terran was reluctant to hand over his own damage report. Tam snatched it from him anyway. With practiced ease, Tam keyed up the last bit—real-time images of the hull of his ship—into the main console. The visuals popping up on the big screen in the bridge were depressing and grim. Tam dropped the tablets onto a chair and slammed one meaty fist onto the console. Terran jumped. Daior growled.

"Gods damn it to the Seventh Ring," Tam bellowed. The gaping holes grinning at them from the monitor would take days to fix. They'd sealed off the far corridors, containing the danger and stabilising the atmosphere in the rest of the cruiser, but they couldn't fly like this. The drag alone would have the metal shearing apart as if cut by a giant pair of scissors.

"We can't risk any of the ports," Daior observed. "We're going to have to repair the hull in shifts. Damn, but I hate spacewalking."

"I'm good at it," Terran said, subdued by the recent attack. "I'm good at repairs, too."

"Absolutely not," Daior snapped. "You're staying in here where it's safe."

Terran didn't point out the obvious. Considering the holes, inside wasn't really any safer than outside. They'd lost the hunters, but who knew how long that would last? If the bastards found them once, they could find them again.

It took them nearly four days to patch the holes in the hull of the cruiser. They ended up welding scrap metal ripped off the inside as a temporary solution and kept those parts of the ship closed down. The cruiser needed extensive repairs before she would be whole again, repairs they simply couldn't do with rigging and suits. And, quite frankly, repairs they weren't good enough to do.

Terran remained in the bridge for most of those four days, watching through the monitors and pouting. He hadn't taken their ultimatum with grace. The second time his lovers found him hanging in space with a welding torch, they'd threatened to lock him in the galley pantry.

Sometimes, overprotective lovers really sucked meteorites.

The gentle, but annoyingly insistent, beep made him shoot upright in his chair. He typed in a few commands, unsure what the ship was upset about.

Tamesis came barrelling around the corner. "Get us out of here!"

Terran began flipping switches, complying with the order even as he felt uncontrollably compelled to ask questions. "What's wrong?"

"Someone's coming out of warp on top of us."

"I didn't think that was possible."

"Oh, it's very possible."

"But I've never—"

"Ships don't normally sit in one spot as long as we have."

"I guess so."

"What *now*?" Daior bellowed the phrase as he stalked through the door, shoulders bunched and hair practically standing on end.

"We have visitors," Tamesis replied.

Terran hit the accelerator. The ship shot forward several hundred metres. Then the engine stalled and their progress halted with a jerk that nearly sent the two standing men tumbling to the floor.

"Seven Gods!" Tam swore.

Terran flicked through the console's main screen. "Damn it! The main power core fried. There must be a shorted wire we missed."

"So we're dead in the water," Tam stated.

"Something like that."

"Please tell me we at least moved out of the drop zone," Dai snapped.

"We moved out of the drop zone." Terran was glad to be able to utter that particular sentence with absolute truth. A mid-space collision was every pilot's worst nightmare. One breech in the hull in the wrong place and instant death. In space, there were no second chances and no rescues.

Terran brought up the large viewing screen. The video flickered slightly before bursting into life. The images spanned nearly the entire front of the ship, long and curved, serving as a front window to the cruiser. It provided a live feed of the area outside with the added advantage of rotation. Terran could use the single screen to visually scan the space all around the ship. Useful for putting a face to the voice, so to speak. It was nice sometimes to be able to see for himself what the sensors were describing.

"You need a new projector," Terran commented. "The picture is pixelating."

"Not the time, baby," Dai replied.

A ship slowly shimmered into view just to the side of them. It was massive, nearly three times wider and at least that much longer than their own little shuttle. A war ship, not a cruiser. Built for deep space travel and prepared to take on any threat.

It was also all too familiar.

"Oh, damn," Terran breathed.

Tam wrapped an arm around him in a comforting embrace. "Who is it, Terran?"

"My brother."

Dai squeezed Terran's shoulder. "Go ahead and hail him, baby," Daior ordered. "Let's see what he wants."

"I know what he wants," Terran snapped. "He wants me."

"Well, he can't have you," Tam said. "So go ahead and tell him that so we can get on with repairs."

"You don't know my brother," Terran insisted. "He doesn't do well with the word 'no'."

"About time he learnt," Dai growled.

That was his fierce grizzly bear. It made Terran smile. He and Tam both knew what lay under the grumpy outside. Unfortunately for Richard, they were the only ones who would ever see that softer side of Dai.

Terran's finger hovered above the button that would open communications. Before he could push it, the familiar beep of an incoming transmission sounded. A small screen popped up inside the larger one, his brother's scowling face staring at him. Terran liked the lines that distorted the image. Made his brother a little less threatening to have a black strip running across his nose.

"You're right," Tam commented. "I do need to replace the projector."

Terran heard the distinctive sound over the connection of a fist meeting flesh. He ignored it.

"Good afternoon, Richard," he said with as much politeness as he could muster. It helped to have the two hulks flanking him.

"Terran, do you have any idea how long it's taken me to track you down?" Richard snapped. "You get your arse back over here right now, young man. You've caused enough trouble."

"I'm staying here," Terran said.

"That wasn't a request!"

"The last time I checked, Terran was an adult." Daior sounded satisfyingly menacing. "I believe you have your answer, so go away."

"You stay out of this. I'll deal with the two of you later."

Tam started to chuckle. "Gods, Bit, he's an arrogant ass." He leaned over to speak the words right into Terran's ear. "Who does he think he is, the king of the universe?"

"Just about."

"Terran!"

Terran suppressed the urge to flinch at his brother's bellow. It wasn't as if his brother would ever hurt him. Richard was just a bit…autocratic. And kind of like a planet's orbit, unstoppable. He bellowed and made a lot of noise and rolled right over everyone, ignoring little things like objections and other people's desires. He was completely convinced he knew what was best for everyone on his ship, Terran in particular. The man was utterly impossible to reason with.

Tam was trying, though.

"We're trained for this sort of situation," his lover was saying. "We can keep him safe."

"Yes, because judging by the holes in your ship, you're doing such a stellar job."

Dai growled.

"That was a miscalculation."

"We've been riding your tail ever since you left that damn compound weeks ago. If you had waited another few hours, we would have rescued Terran ourselves. And left a pile of rubble behind."

"And Daior?" Terran asked.

His brother ignored the question, which was really all the answer Terran needed. His brother would have pulled Terran out, and only Terran. Anyone else would have been left to rot. Terran supposed he should be comforted by the fact his brother was so focussed on his safety.

He wasn't.

"We've been tracking you across galaxies ever since. And if we've been tracking you, I can guarantee that so have the others. They found you once and they can find you again. You can only run for so long."

"And you think you can protect him?"

"I know I can."

"Hey, I'm right here!" Terran protested. Tam gave his shoulder another squeeze but he ignored it. "I don't want to go back with you, Richard. We'll manage just fine."

"I promised Father nothing would happen to you, and I intend to keep that promise," Richard snapped. "I have the manpower and firepower to eliminate any threat."

"Then how did they get their hands on him in the first place?" Dai asked.

That question earned Terran a really vicious glare. "Little brother sneaked off the ship. Again. By the time we realised he wasn't where he was supposed to be, it was too late."

"And what's to keep that from happening again?" Tam asked reasonably.

"It won't," Richard said with harsh conviction.

Terran swivelled around to see the faces of his two guys when the silence started to grow. He gasped.

"You're actually considering this," he accused.

Guilty silence greeted him. Terran shot from his chair, hair standing on end and so mad he could just spit. Mad and hurt. Gods, it hurt.

"You said we were a team," he said. "That you would take care of me. That you *cared* about me!"

Tam called Terran's name and reached out, attempting to soothe him. Terran danced out of reach.

"You can't do this."

"I swore to protect you," Dai said.

"So protect me! You can't do that if I'm on one side of the galaxy and you're on the other."

"Sometimes caring about someone means doing something they may not like. For their own good."

Just like Richard, Dai didn't appear to hear his protests. *Fantastic.* Another person who thought they knew best. That Terran was just a stupid little brat who didn't know his head from his arse.

"Don't talk to me like I'm twelve," Terran shouted. "You may not have a high opinion of my intellectual capacity, but I know what I want. I want to stay here with you. I don't want to leave. Please, don't make me leave."

At this point Terran was begging, a pleading note in his voice. He didn't care. He hurt, from head to feet. Ached at the thought of leaving his men behind. Maybe they weren't acting like it right now, but they cared about him. Maybe even loved him. They were the first men to find out about his peculiarities and not give a darn.

And Terran loved the two stubborn jerks. In the end, that was all that really mattered. No way was Terran going to give them up.

Tam sighed. "Terran, go pack your things."

Terran swung his disbelieving gaze to Tam. "Not you, too," he whispered.

Dai grabbed his shoulders and turned him, ducking down so they were face to face. "Just until we can take care of the threat, baby," he said. "We need you to be safe. You hold us together, remember?"

"No." The word didn't hold much conviction. Terran could see it in Dai's eyes, in both their eyes. They'd made up their minds and they weren't going to be swayed by anything he said. "Don't do this, please. Let me stay. I just want to stay."

Tam folded Terran into a hug from behind, pinning his smaller body between their bulky frames. Terran closed his eyes for a second, relishing the feel of them surrounding and engulfing him.

Then Dai stepped away, and Terran's world shattered. He reached out for the dark form of his lover, unable to hold back a small whimper.

"Just until you're safe," Dai promised. "Then we'll come find you. I swear."

"Listen to him, Bit," Tam murmured into his ear, arms still wrapped around Terran's shoulders. "Dai always keeps his promises. You know that."

"I don't want to go." But Terran knew they weren't listening to him anymore. His heart fractured, the pain ripping apart his insides like a sharp knife. From deep inside him something stirred. The cat part of Terran let out a long, anguished howl.

He wanted to echo it out loud. As he lifted his gaze from the floor and met Richard's triumphant smile, he knew.

Terran wasn't going to see his men again.

Far too soon, Terran found himself standing in the airlock, clutching his small backpack of clothes and medicine to his chest. Dai and Tam stood in front of him, broad shoulders brushing, unreadable expressions on their faces. Terran clamped his lips closed around more pleas. It wouldn't help. The only people he'd ever met who could outdo him in stubbornness were standing in his view.

The airlock door slowly hissed shut, separating them with a piece of glass and steel. He watched their faces through the small window for as long as possible, until gentle hands took his arm and pulled him backwards.

Terran looked up into Jackson's sympathetic face. Hot tears slid down Terran's cheeks, tears he didn't try to hold back.

Jackson gave his upper arm a small squeeze and led him through the matching airlock and onto his brother's ship. Terran didn't look back again, knowing it would only hurt more. And he couldn't take any more hurt. He just wanted to find some dark corner and lick away his wounds. Or at least try to ease them. Because these wounds? They weren't ever going to heal.

Richard was waiting for them, arms crossed over his chest, looking far too smug for Terran's peace of mind. Terran wanted to scream, rage, but he couldn't find the energy. So he just stared at his brother until Richard's arms dropped to his sides, until concern replaced superiority.

"It's for the best, Terran," Richard defended. "And if you looked at it rationally, you'd realise that."

Terran shook his head. "Just leave me alone," he whispered.

Layna stepped up beside him, sympathy in her eyes, and touched his shoulder. "Terran, why don't we go get—"

Terran shoved her hand away. His pack hit the floor and he ran. He didn't know where he was going—it wasn't like there really *was* any place to go. He didn't care. Terran had to get away from Richard.

He ran through the hallways, dodging crewmembers. Ran until he realised it wasn't helping, that he wasn't going to be able to outrun the pain.

Then he found one of his favourite cubbyholes, wrapped his arms around his knees and sobbed.

# Chapter Twenty

Terran curled himself into a little ball, trying to wedge himself farther into the corner. He didn't bother trying to wipe away the tears that still stubbornly slipped down his cheeks. His stomach ached and his head hurt and he just wanted to go *home.*

Too bad he didn't know where that would be.

He heard footsteps in the hall and his brother's voice calling for him. He wrapped his arms around his head, covering his ears. *Not coming out. Don't want to. Go away.* He was just going to stay here in his hiding place until the world disappeared.

They'd left him. Just turned around and walked away, leaving him with his brother. He wasn't helpless, damn it. And he wasn't a child, even if he wanted to act like one, throw a tantrum and scream his denial. He knew what he wanted. And he wanted his men. Here, not halfway across the galaxy in some misguided attempt to protect him. He needed them.

And they needed him. Whether they would admit to it or not.

Eventually, hunger drove him from his small shelter. It was late—or early. It was always hard to tell in space. The corridors were empty, the rooms he passed silent and dark.

Terran grabbed a quick snack from the nearest food generator, which happened to be conveniently located in one of the three communication centres on the massive ship.

Richard's *Celsius* completely dwarfed Tam's little cruiser. With three decks and a crew of over eighty specialists, it was more like a floating fortress. Complete with bristling weaponry.

Richard Praetis was a merchant for their home planet. Well, 'merchant' was perhaps not quite the right term. They transported necessary supplies for the government and handled diplomatic matters at the same time. The Praetis family was a powerful one, active in all levels of government. Richard and Terran had both been trained from an early age in interplanetary relations and diplomacy.

Terran hadn't listened. Richard only applied it when absolutely necessary and never bothered when it came to family.

Their father wasn't exactly pleased with the results of the expensive education in either of his children.

With thoughts of his father bouncing around his head, Terran settled himself in a chair. He munched on a soggy French fry and dialled in the code to reach his family home.

It wasn't until the screen flickered on to reveal a very sleepy-eyed butler that Terran gave any thought to what time it probably was back home.

"Sorry, Kesselar," he said with a sheepish shrug, the best he could muster. "I don't suppose my father's available?"

"It's four-thirty in the morning, Master Terran. No, he is not," came the tart reply.

"I don't suppose you'd be willing to wake him up?"

"No need," an amused voice said from behind Kesselar's stiffly set shoulders. "I'm here. Go back to bed, Kesselar."

"Very good, Sir."

The familiar deep brown eyes and craggy features of his father's face appeared in Kesselar's place. Some of Terran's tension leaked away at the welcome sight. Even though they hadn't been in the same physical location for more than three years, Terran and his father were very close. It was comforting, just seeing the man whose steady presence had been such a constant force in Terran's life.

Evan Praetis sat at the console with a heavy sigh. "What has your brother done now?" he asked.

It was a logical question. Most of the time when Terran called, it was with a complaint about Richard.

Richard hadn't always been such a stuck-up jerk. Once upon a time, he'd actually been a decent brother. Terran was never sure what had happened to change all that. He just knew that when Richard had come back from his first trip off-planet, he'd been different. After that, Richard had spent most of his time in space and Terran hadn't seen much of him, so it hadn't mattered. Until Terran had turned fifteen and they'd sent him to live with Richard.

Terran had been devastated at the time, leaving everything familiar, leaving his parents. Time and maturity had given him an altered view. He could admit now that his parents hadn't been given much choice.

Until Terran's teenage years, he'd been pretty normal. Any anomalies were easily hidden. But when he hit puberty—far later than most—certain peculiarities had begun to make themselves known. His canine teeth had lengthened into small points, his hair had developed light stripes in the ginger depths and the mood swings had worsened to the point that the medication had become necessary. Due to the constant scrutiny the Praetis family was always under, it was decided Terran would be safer away from the planet and in a more…isolated setting.

There were more than a few fanatics who believed anyone showing hints of splicing to be an abomination. If it had just been worry about a fall-out for his political career, Terran had no doubt Evan would have told the general population to go jump off a cliff. It had been the actual, physical danger to his son that caused him concern.

"It wasn't really Richard this time, at least not completely," Terran said, pulling himself from his thoughts to answer his father's question.

Evan waited patiently for the rest of the story.

It wasn't long in coming. Terran poured out everything, starting from when he'd gone down to an entertainment planet to, well, find some entertainment, and been kidnapped. It took him nearly half an hour to get the explanation out. Everything. He didn't leave any details out. Well, maybe some, but Terran probably did tell his father more about his recent sex life than Evan cared to hear about.

When Terran wound to an end, Evan studied him with serious eyes.

"Son, why are you there?"

"What?"

"I've always worried about you, you know," Evan said. "Worried you wouldn't find someone who could accept you. Instead, you surprise me, as you always do, and find two."

"It doesn't…bother you?"

Evan shook his head. "Love is precious. It's clear to me that you love these two men. I've always believed feelings are stronger when shared. It's certainly not my place to judge. Besides, it would be hypocritical of me. There's a lot about my younger years I don't share with my children."

"And I prefer it that way," Terran said quickly.

"My point here is this—I've always admired your insistence on pursuing your dreams. You've always known what you wanted and have never hesitated to push until you grasped your goals. So why now, when it really matters, are you giving up?"

Terran opened his mouth to protest then closed it again when he realised his father was right. He *had* given up. It was true, the guys would probably have just picked him up and tossed him onto the *Celsius*, anyway. But he had acquiesced, hadn't fought until the end.

Terran nodded decisively to himself. It wasn't too late to fight, not as long as all three of them were still alive.

He gave his father a brilliant grin that easily conveyed his resolve even across the thousands of light years separating them.

"See, that's why I call you," Terran said. "You always give good advice."

"Tell that to the current Regent," Evan replied dryly.

Terran laughed, his spirit feeling pounds lighter than it had earlier that day. "I have no doubt that whatever issue you're championing this time, you'll win out in the end. You always do. It's a particular talent of the Praetis family."

"So are you going to put that talent to good use?"

"Absolutely. Just don't tell Richard."

Evan chuckled. "No, I'll let you boys work out your differences on your own. Just don't get so wrapped up in your new life that you forget to call now and then."

"Never," Terran declared. "Say hi to Mom for me and I'll let you know how it all turns out."

"You do that."

Terran cut the connection and stretched, mind already busy forming a plan.

Operation Reunion was going to take skill, stubbornness and more than a little luck.

He couldn't wait to get started.

* * * *

Tam looked up with a frown when Dai stomped into the kitchen, fury etched in the tight muscles of his body.

"Found it." Dai tossed a little piece of plastic onto the table, scowling fiercely. "Go ahead and say it. I'm a fucking idiot and so out of practice it's pitiful."

"What the hell are you going on about?" Tam asked around a mouthful of cereal. He used the end of his spoon to poke at the item in question. "What is this?"

"Tracking device." The disgust in Dai's voice was almost thick enough to see.

"You're joking."

"Wish I was. I got to wondering how the hell they kept catching up to us. I finally hit on the brilliant idea of running a bug scan on myself. Found that."

"When—"

"Damned if I know," Dai interrupted with disgust. "They probably planted it on me back at the compound. There's a couple of hours in there that are a bit fuzzy."

"So they've known right where we were the whole time."

"Pretty much. Guess we've just been moving too fast for them to pin us down."

"You know, if you've got one, it's a good bet they tagged Terran, too."

"I know. Gods take it." Dai's voice radiated with barely-suppressed anger.

Hell, Tam was just impressed the other man was managing to suppress anything.

Tam grunted and pushed back from the small, four person table. Square and made of highly polished wood, it was shoved into one corner of their compact kitchen. Tam crossed the room in a few strides, feet silent on the vinyl floor, and dropped his ceramic bowl into the sink. Milk and little round 'o's still floated in the bottom, but he wasn't hungry anymore.

"I guess that's something, anyway. That even with their edge, we were still staying a few steps ahead of them."

"Yeah. Sure. Real comforting."

Tam sighed and headed out of the room, back towards the bridge. Daior stayed close on his heels.

"It'll make the next part easier," Tam pointed out. As soon as Terran had vanished from sight, they'd begun making plans. A few tweaks had the *Farion* operational again, at least enough to get them to the nearest mechanic for some finishing work.

Now it was time to go on the offensive. They'd been playing tag for far, far too long. Both Dai and Tam were ready to take the battle to the bad guys. With Terran safe, they could proceed without worrying.

Of course, the worry had been replaced with different, more dangerous, emotions. Tam was beginning to think they should have kept their mouths shut and told Richard to go jump into space.

"I still think we should head for Tandy, then work our way through the Ellis Sector," Dai said. He leaned over Tam's shoulder, staring at the map lit up on the screen in front of them. "We're dealing with Malkaians. They'd go towards the Fringe."

"But they're being paid, and money comes from the Centre," Tam pointed out.

It had taken both Dai and Tam, brainstorming together, to realise why the mercenaries following them, and the guards at the facility, all had looked so familiar. Each one had the stamp of a Malkaian. The Malkaians were an extended family, operating out of a massive transport ship they'd converted into a mini-Spacestation. They hung around the fringes of space, each and every one highly-trained and highly-equipped. And available for a price.

With that realisation, it hadn't taken long for Tam to conclude they were most likely dealing with a single, private funding source rather than a government. A government would have options—they wouldn't stoop to hiring Malkaian mercenaries. It had been

Tam's opinion they follow the money, as the saying went.

Space had been colonised from Earth on out. The planets in the surrounding galaxies were well-developed and highly populated. Modern and civilised. The farther one got in space, the cruder civilisation became.

Anyone with money would be near the Centre, living a life of luxury.

"But the Fringe is—" Dai began.

Tam's temper snapped. Daior had been riding him for hours now, and he'd had enough.

"Would you shut up already!" Tam bellowed. "I thought we agreed on a course two days ago. What the hell is wrong with you?"

Daior growled, a long, drawn-out sound that worked its way up from his toes. "Same thing that's wrong with you," he snapped.

"Don't you dare start with me." Tam's anger abruptly subsided, deflating like an untied balloon. He dropped into the co-pilot's chair and scrubbed one hand over his face. "We made a mistake," he said quietly.

Dai didn't—or more likely pretended not to—hear, busying himself with flipping switches that didn't need to be flipped. The expressionless mask he wore didn't fool Tam for a second.

"We both know it," he persisted. He'd known, the instant they'd watched the *Celsius* fade away. Terran belonged with them, not floating through space with his overbearing ass of a brother.

Dai groaned. "What if we did? What do you want to do about it? It's too late. Terran's half way to Earth by now. Even if we could catch up, his brother isn't just going to hand him back to us with an understanding smile."

"Must you always be so negative?"

"Yes."

The silence between them grew, thick and heavy. And awkward. Ever since Terran had left, the silences were increasingly awkward.

"I hate to admit it," Dai finally said, "But you were right. We need Terran. Need him to hold us together."

"Our gooey centre," Tam murmured.

"Yeah."

"Damn, but we're pathetic bastards. We didn't even last a week."

It was true. Tam loved Dai, heart and soul. But love wasn't always enough. The two of them alone just didn't work. Already their relationship was falling apart. They were too much alike. They needed their little cat to complete them, to hold the whole mess together. Without Terran, the best Tam could ever hope for with Dai would be work partners. And even that was a bit iffy, because he couldn't be around the man for long without wanting him. A lot. They did okay with the sex, but the rest of it? Not so much.

"All right," Dai finally growled. "I give up. Where do you think the *Celsius* went?"

"My best guess would be—"

The persistent beeping of an alarm hailed an incoming signal.

"Well, well," Dai said. "Speak of the devil and he appears."

The familiar bulk of the *Celsius* shimmered into view in front of them as the ship dropped out of warp. Within the large front screen, a smaller window opened up to show Richard, standing with arms crossed and a characteristic scowl on his face.

"Where is my brother?" Richard snapped.

"With you," Tam snapped back. "Right where we left him."

Richard dropped his arms to his sides, his face dropping with them. "You mean you don't have him? He's not with you?"

"What the hell are you jabbering about?" Dai snarled.

An older man in uniform, taller than Richard but without his bulk, separated himself from the crowd milling about behind Richard. He placed one hand on Richard's shoulder and nodded a greeting. At the touch, Richard lost some of his bristle.

"What I believe the captain here is trying to ask is whether or not you have heard from Terran anytime in the last several days."

"No," Tam replied. If this guy were willing to play nice, so could he. At least until they got themselves some solid answers.

"Then we might have a bit of a problem."

"It's not a problem," Richard said.

Whether Richard was trying to convince Tam or himself wasn't clear, but the whole conversation was putting Tam on edge.

"Now that I know he isn't with you, we'll just be on our way," Richard continued.

"Oh, no you don't," Tam warned. "You can't just pop in like that, ask leading questions then take off again without any explanations."

"Richard, I'll handle this," the lanky man said. There was a sharp tone in his voice, almost scolding. "You've screwed up enough with Terran already."

Richard opened his mouth to protest but the man squeezed his arm, cutting off the words.

"What about Terran?" Dai's question was nearly bellowed. Dai wasn't the most patient of men even at the best of times. And this was certainly not the best of times.

"It seems we've lost him," Richard replied. The look on his face indicated the words were actually painful for him to get out.

"What do you mean, you've 'lost him'?" Dai's voice was deadly calm, his jaw set.

*Damn.* The last time Tam had seen Dai that angry was during that far too memorable fight. His arm still ached like a bitch whenever he was on a planet with damp weather.

Richard should consider himself very, very lucky to be delivering this particular news over a vidscreen instead of in person.

Tam wasn't exactly pleased, himself. "How long has Terran been missing?"

Richard paused, and even over the not-quite-clear screen his reluctance was visible.

"How long, *Dick*?" Dai demanded through gritted teeth and clenched jaw.

"I'm not certain. We found the crawlspace he'd been hiding in, but I can't tell how long it's been unoccupied."

"Crawlspace?" Tam asked, wrinkling his brow in mixed confusion and concern.

Richard shook his head, very much the quintessential aggravated older sibling. "He was mad at me. Terran is always mad at me. And when he's mad, he finds a spot and holes up. It usually takes my crew a couple of days to locate him, even with the scanners. The brat can get himself into the blasted tiniest places."

"Of course he can," Dai replied scathingly. "He's a cat."

"We don't mention that!"

"Which is a stupid attitude," Tam pointed out with very little patience. "He's part cat, after all. It seems to me when you ignore that pertinent fact, you get into trouble with Terran. Where was your last stop?"

"Yesterday, in Paramount. But the day before we hit three ports on Cardwin."

"Damn it, did you have to make a jump between the two?"

*Shit, that made it harder. Much harder.* The Cardwin ports saw a lot of shuttle activity and were nowhere near Paramount Station. Terran could, quite literally, be anywhere in the galaxy by now. Hell, if he got off at the first Cardwin port, he could be anywhere in two galaxies. Maybe three, if he took the right transport.

"We'll find him," Tam reassured, more for himself and Dai than Terran's arsehole brother.

"I'm sure you will," Richard's companion replied calmly. "And I trust that when you do, you'll inform us. I'll assure his family he is safe and protected."

"Damn right," Dai snarled. "And ours. This time, we won't be giving him back."

"I didn't think you would." The officer remained completely unperturbed, giving Dai and Tam a brief, acknowledging nod. "I'll send over the coordinates from when we know for certain that Terran was last on the ship. I'll also give you a copy of our flight route. From there, I imagine your sources will be more useful than ours."

"Thank you," Tam said.

"You're most welcome. Good luck."

The screen slid away, leaving only an uninterrupted view of the *Celsius*.

"Interesting man," Tam remarked.

"Can I kill Richard?"

"No."

"Damn."

Tam ignored him, busy scrolling through the information streaming through to their systems. As promised, it contained everything regarding the *Celsius's* route.

"Here," Tam said, pointing at the line of text he'd paused on the monitor. "I think Terran probably jumped ship at the second port on Cardwin. It's got the widest route spread. And multiple direct flights to Indara. Check for any shuttles that might have left within the hour after the *Celsius* docked."

"You think he's looking for us." It was a statement, not a question. Dai was already busy at his own monitor, checking the schedules in Cardwin.

"Yes. And even if he isn't, he's going to go for the familiar. Besides that, his medicine will run out eventually. He'll need to find Marvin."

Tam shoved Dai aside, taking his spot at the console. A quick check, and he turned the nose towards Cardwin.

Dai took the co-pilot's seat this time. "I'll make some calls," he said. "Let's just go find our baby."

"You got it."

The *Farion* shot off, quickly reaching lightspeed and leaving the *Celsius*—and Richard—far behind.

# Chapter Twenty-One

Terran slipped into the mass of humanity—and the not so human.

"This is really, monumentally stupid," he muttered to himself, dodging a purple guy with three arms. Looked unbalanced as hell to him. Nature had goofed on that one. Although, in this part of the galaxy, nature might not have had much to do with it.

He made his way quickly along the gleaming walkway, cursing himself the entire way. He might as well just paint a big red X on his back and wave a flag with his name on it. He had a feeling his pursuers were going to be on him within hours.

Uneasiness swirled in his gut, a premonition that the whole plan was going to go horribly awry. He was itchy and growly and the medicine didn't seem to be keeping the mood swings under control. He was too on edge. Terran needed his guys. And if they weren't going to come to him then, by all that was holy—and all that was unholy, too—he was going to go to them. Now. No matter what anyone said.

And with the mood he was in, Gods help the idiot who got in his way. The vicious thought was strangely satisfying, and Terran nodded decisively to himself, garnering several sideways looks. Or maybe that was because of the way he kept muttering under his breath. *Yeah, that probably has more to do with it. Too bad.*

He showed his teeth to someone who stared a bit too long. They backed off with satisfying speed. He licked his fangs and kept moving.

Terran's goal was a small freighter in Dock six-point-three-five-two, the only flight he'd been able to book. Damn slow method of travel, but he didn't want to linger on Cardwin where Richard—or anyone else—might think to look for him. The slug boat would take him to the nearby planet of Minorus. Which was, not surprisingly, a large mining planet. Lots of transport ships docked there, and most of them would take on a passenger or two, especially for the right price. Having emptied a large portion of his brother's main bank account, Terran could most definitely afford that right price. The plan was to head to Indara. Hopefully, Marvin could give him a heads-up on where Tam might go.

It was a start, anyway. Of course, Terran wasn't adverse to the blinding strike of inspiration, either.

Inspiration struck him with blunt—and for once unwelcome—force a few minutes after he alighted on Minorus. It came in the unlikely form of four sleek figures in partial body armour, carrying an impressive amount of weaponry.

Oh, he was so not in the mood for this. Although, it was gratifying to see the extra man. Meant they'd made an impression on someone, anyway.

The tallest mercenary laid one hand on the butt of a gun strapped to his hip. "Are you going to come easily, little cat?"

"No," Terran replied, curling his lip.

"Not wise," another added. "You're only going to get hurt."

"Maybe," Terran said. "But I'll take some chunks of you with me."

He didn't wait, just launched himself at the tall guy. They went down in a tangle of arms and legs, yowling and yelling. Terran hissed violently and threw his whole body into the fight, slamming his fist into the nearest body part he could reach.

Luckily enough, it was the tall guy's head. As he was helmetless, the blow to the temple dropped him limply to the pavement. Terran didn't hesitate, diving for the next man's legs. He wrapped his fingers around booted ankles and yanked, knocking Number Two off-balance. The guy reached for him, but Terran sank his fangs into his hand with satisfying results.

The third man grabbed Terran around the waist and pulled him off his fallen companion. Terran wriggled and squirmed. He managed to land a solid kick to the man's upper thigh. The tight grip loosened, and Terran slid down enough to get another kick onto the man's knee. Number Three's legs buckled, and Terran slammed his boot up. The man was going down, Terran's leg was going up, and the two forces connected right at Number Three's balls. The man hit the ground, gasping and sobbing for air.

The last man was closing in, so Terran whirled and made a run for it. He dashed around a pile of crates, not bothering to look back even when he heard the sound of feet in pursuit. He ducked between two parked transports and rounded a corner.

Terran slammed face-first into a hard and unyielding surface.

"Hell!" he shouted, staggering backwards.

Strong hands grabbed his arms and hoisted him off his feet. Terran looked up. And up some more.

*Dang.* And he'd thought Tam was big. This guy was like a freaking mountain. Seven feet tall at least, all distorted, bulging muscle and no neck. Terran squirmed but he might as well have been trying to pull apart a pneumatic clamp with his bare hands. No give at all.

Two of the men who'd accosted him came barrelling around the corner, faces red with exertion and anger.

"Lose something?" the big guy asked.

"Damn bastard is quick," Number One said in a defensive voice.

"And you're slow," was the reply. "Come on, the boss is waiting."

Terran screamed and kicked and squirmed, but it didn't do any good. No one paid any attention as he was hauled through the streets.

At least he could take some satisfaction in the fact that two of his assailants never showed up and one of the ones lagging behind moved gingerly. It was something, anyway.

Terran was tiring, but he kept up his assault for five whole blocks. When they reached block six, an old-style transport vehicle rumbled past them. A loud backfire, complete with dark smoke, burst from the tailpipe.

It distracted his captors, all of them flinching and whirling as if expecting an attack. Terran seized his chance. He twisted free and ran for all he was worth.

They caught him within another five blocks. By this point, Terran was breathing hard and dang, but he was sore. Everywhere.

"For the love of the Gods," Big Idiot growled. "This is just fuckin' ridiculous."

"I agree," Terran sniped. They had him backed into a corner. He could feel his hair standing on end and knew he probably looked like an utter mess. "So why don't we call it a draw and go our separate ways?"

"Not happening, you little bitch. We were hired to bring you in, and that's what we're going to do."

The big man swept in and grabbed Terran around the waist. Terran yelled when another one grabbed his arms.

They didn't tie him up, but Terran found himself effectively caged in muscular arms and pressed tightly against even more muscular bodies.

*Well, hell.* Looked like he'd lost. But that didn't mean he had to like it, he thought, growling low in his chest.

Number Two jumped out of range.

"Watch the teeth," he advised. "They're painful."

"Wuss," muttered the guy holding Terran.

Terran smiled grimly.

They limped into an empty warehouse a few minutes later, the massive guy literally carrying Terran under one arm. Big Idiot hadn't taken his companion's advice—blood dripped from distinctive teeth marks on his hand. Terran squirmed and tried to aim another punch at the idiot's side. Someone smacked his bum for his trouble

Terran let out a yowl of protest and bared his teeth, hissing furiously. Only Dai and Tam got to touch his arse. In any way. Terran shifted his weight back and launched a leg out to the side.

*Score!* His foot connected with something solid and yielding. The man let out a short cry of pain.

"Settle down, kitten," Big Idiot snarled.

"Then put me down," Terran snarled back.

"And have you bite me again? Not a chance. I think I'm gonna have to get a rabies shot as it is."

Terran hissed again.

"Problems, gentlemen?"

Terran stilled, eyes squinting through the gloom of the rundown warehouse for this new threat. A tall, lean man dressed impeccably—and improbably—in a white, three-piece suit stepped into the narrow beam of light filtering through one of the high, dusty windows.

"Nothing we couldn't handle," Big Idiot answered.

With casual disregard, the man dropped Terran. Terran hit the floor hard, sprawling on his hands and knees.

"So it's true," the man mused, studying Terran's position. "Cats do land on their feet."

"Fuck you," Terran snarled, shoving himself upright.

"Sorry, you're not my type."

"Let me guess," Terran said, curling his lip in irritation, knowing it would nicely showcase his tiny fangs. "Erasmus Carter?"

"Nice to know you're not just a pretty face." Erasmus Carter, Lord Protector of Marquos, did an admirable job of hiding his emotions, but a hint of surprise showed in his eyes. Bastard thought he was so far superior to everyone else that it never occurred to him that other people had brains. And used them, too.

Terran had had a lot of time to think while hidden away on the *Celsius.* The one thing he had always kept coming back to was the choice to kidnap Daior. Terran understood snatching the little splice—he was unique, and he knew it. But Dai? It had never made any sense to Terran. There were other Teks in the universe, a lot of other Teks. And while Dai and Tam might be unique in their own way, the basic design work was still the same.

It had started him thinking that maybe there was a personal aspect to this whole blinking mess. As soon as he'd seen the suit, Terran had known what was really going on. After all, there weren't that many people in the universe arrogant enough to wander around what was basically a pirate port wearing a white suit.

Two, in fact. One was the president of the Naturide Federation, and he rarely left the council building. That left Carter, scum of the universe.

Terran said as much. Unfortunately, his opinion just seemed to amuse the cocky bastard.

"Yes, it is a very nice suit, isn't it?" Carter tugged on his lapels. Honest to the Gods, the man even preened a bit.

"That wasn't a compliment, jerkwad," Terran said.

Carter crossed the room in three strides. He struck Terran across the cheek with the back of his hand, catching Terran completely off guard. Terran staggered sideways from the force of the blow.

Spitting, Terran focussed his meanest glare on the man. "You really are an idiot, messing with Tam and Dai. They'll eat you for lunch."

"Not if they can't get to me," Carter said, waving his hand dismissively. "And by the time they find out you were here, we'll be long gone."

"You found me," Terran pointed out. "So will they."

"Ah, but I had more than luck and logic on my side," Carter said with a satisfied smirk. "I had bribery and manipulation. It was a simple enough matter to ensure I knew who got on what transports. It was even easier to make sure you booked passage on the flight I wanted. It brought you right to me. Your dear mercenary friends won't have the same advantage."

Terran growled and went for the bastard again. Strong hands once more jerked him to a stop.

"Enough. Lock him up," Carter ordered. "I have other business to conclude before we can leave. And keep an eye on him. He gets away again, and I'm taking it out of your hides."

The three big men looked vaguely queasy at the threat. Hell, Terran was feeling a bit queasy, himself. He could see it now, beneath that well-groomed, well-bred exterior. The lurking madness and utter disregard for anyone's well-being aside from his own. Terran was looking at a true, textbook definition sociopath.

He didn't bother to fight much as they dragged him across the barren, concrete floor. No point, really. Besides, the farther he got away from Carter, the better.

His captors stopped in front of a rusty door. It let out an ear-splitting squeal when Big Idiot jerked it open.

They shoved him in. Terran went, but not without one last hiss.

He found himself standing in gloom. The slamming of the door behind him cut off all but the faintest light, and Terran growled.

*Great, just great.*

Looked like Operation Reunion had hit a snag.

# Chapter Twenty-Two

Terran paced the confines of the tiny room, more of a closet, really. His eyes adjusted quickly to the dimness, letting him navigate the scattered piles of junk with ease. *Damn, damn, and triple damn.*

He needed to calm down, to think for a minute. No way was he going to sit here and wait for someone to rescue him. Not this time. He was through with that. His guys, they loved him, but they thought he was helpless. So did his brother. It was about time they learnt that, little and scattered though he was, he could still take care of himself. Sometimes. If he tried really hard.

"Okay, enough with the pep talk," he told himself, listening to the way his voice echoed in the tiny space. The pep talk was just depressing him, anyway.

Terran stopped pacing and started looking. He walked alongside the walls, tracing every crack and space with sharp eyes and fingers, searching for something, anything, that might give him a way out.

Because just as he wasn't going to wait around for someone to rescue him, he also wasn't going to wait around for whatever Mr Suit had in mind. And he really, really wasn't going to let Carter use him against the guys.

And that, Terran thought, was the ultimate plan.

It hadn't started out that way, he knew that. At first, it was just a greedy bastard trying to put together a super-soldier project. Terran was the only splice around, at least that he knew of. And for someone as twisted as Carter, the rest would have been a simple choice. He needed Teks to examine, high-class Teks. And it just so happened he had a grudge against a pair of Teks currently wandering the galaxy, alone and vulnerable.

Dai would have been the logical choice. Not only had he shut down his technological aspects, making him an easier target, but Carter was a twisted fucker. The one he really hated, above anything, was Tam. And anyone who knew anything about Tam knew his weak point was Daior, his former partner and lover.

Now Terran was the weak point for both Daior and Tamesis. And Terran knew Carter wasn't about to give up the opportunity to exploit that point for all it was worth.

So, escape. Then find his guys and warn them. Anything after that? He'd just have to wait and see what happened.

There, near the ceiling.

Terran hadn't been idle during his inner monologue, and it paid off now. At the jointure of wall and ceiling on the outer right corner of the room was a glint of metal. An air vent. Uncovered, to boot. It was tiny. Really tiny. Probably why the Idiot Trio hadn't given it a second thought. Because no way could a man fit through the space.

Fortunately, Terran wasn't a man. Not entirely, anyway.

There was an empty crate by the door and Terran shoved it into position under the vent. He backed up as far as the room would allow him, which wasn't very far. But it should do.

He took a deep breath and launched into a run. He bounded off the crate and used his momentum to propel his body up the wall, jumping for the opening. He managed to hook his fingertips over the edge.

Then let go.

Terran landed on his back with enough impact to see actual stars. He lay there for far too long, trying to get the air back into his lungs.

Okay, so the first time hadn't worked. Didn't mean he was ready to give up.

Once the room stopped spinning and his lungs started working properly, Terran gave it another shot. Take off the heavy boots, speed across the room, launch off the crate, push off the wall, grab the top of the vent opening.

This time he found enough purchase for his fingers to vault himself feet-first into the space.

Damn, he really would have preferred head-first. *Oh, well.* He'd take what he could get. At least he had made it.

It took a lot of wriggling and squirming. A whole lot. Because damn, the vent was tiny. Almost too much even for him. But somehow he managed to slide himself inside, and damn if he knew how that worked. He never did. His brother would always find him in these insanely tiny spaces and wonder how the hell he fit. Terran's reply was always that he didn't know, he just did.

Terran figured it was one of those things in life that was just better to accept instead of trying to puzzle through.

He slid along the cold metal, trying desperately to be quiet. And trying equally desperately to think of wide open spaces. He normally liked small cubbyholes, but this was ridiculous.

It was dark in the vent, dark and cold. And it smelt funny, like they didn't run their purification system very often. Which they probably didn't. It looked like the warehouse wasn't used for much these days.

Much besides holding people prisoner, that is.

Every time he slid forward, his shirt rucked up a little more beneath him until he was sliding along cold metal in his bare skin. The metal tried to grab and stick. It was a huge relief when he started to sweat. At least then he slid better.

It seemed like hours later, but was probably only several minutes, when Terran spotted the proverbial light at the end of the tunnel over the tips of his toes. He wanted to make some snide comment but bit his tongue in time, reminding himself firmly he was trying to be *quiet*.

Now came the tough part. If his sense of distance and direction were correct—and he really wasn't willing to bet they were—he should be back in the main room.

Terran hadn't the slightest idea who might be waiting for him on the other side of the open vent. Hell, for all he knew, he could drop down and keep going, falling right off the edge of the building. But he couldn't stay in here forever.

Terran closed his eyes briefly, gathering his nerve. At the very least, this was going to hurt.

Then he braced his hands on the walls by his waist, shoved hard and launched himself out of the opening.

* * * *

Tam hit the lock on their little cruiser, activating the security systems, before he jogged down the small ramp to where Daior waited impatiently.

"All set," he said.

"Now we just have to hope we guessed right."

"We guessed right," Tam replied with a confidence he really didn't feel.

They stood, shoulder to shoulder, arms folded, studying their surroundings with identical focus. It was just like the old days, just like the last ten years had never happened. Tam thought with wry amusement that they still made one hell of a team. Probably always would. He supposed that was what happened when you were physically, genetically and technologically altered to partner with someone.

Or maybe it was just them. Either way, he felt his confidence growing. Yeah, if Terran were anywhere on this planet? They'd find him. And if he weren't, they'd keep looking until they did find him. Either way, they were getting their little lover back. In one piece and unscathed. Or things might get bloody.

"I don't suppose you chipped him?" Tam asked.

His question was met with a disbelieving snort. "When would I have had the time? We were too busy fucking like rabbits."

"That's kind of a nasty image."

Silence. Tam pressed, "So, did you chip him?" He was familiar with Dai's answer-that-isn't-an-answer routine, and there had been a lot of sarcasm in Dai's earlier statement.

"Yeah," Dai admitted. "But you only had a short-range transmitter. I'll need to be within a quarter mile to pick him up."

"Hell, that's kind of pointless. Remind me to find something better. Preferably one that you can pick up within several galaxies."

"Yeah. I get the feeling we'll need it sooner rather than later."

With no other options, they started walking. Not that they didn't have a plan. Tam figured they'd head for the market district, find the nearest pub and start intimidating the hell out of people. It was usually the fastest way to get information.

They wove their way through the streets in tandem, muscles gliding smoothly, systems humming with anticipation. Tam set his scanners for maximum range, knowing Dai would be doing the same. Their processing chips would pick up any threat long before any biological instincts could kick in, even their enhanced ones.

Just past the hustle and crowds of the port, Dai came to a stop. His head swivelled, eyes closed, listening carefully to that inner voice that Tam knew with equal familiarity. Same damn woman had recorded both of their programming. She had the most irritating voice. Or maybe that was just because he'd been forced to listen to her for the last thirty odd years.

Tam waited in patient silence for Dai to process whatever information he was receiving.

Dai's eyes fluttered open and turned towards him, green sparks streaking in their dark depths, his systems working overtime.

"Got him," Dai drawled with complete satisfaction. "Warehouse, next block over."

They started to run, ignoring any startled looks tossed their way.

*Condition?* Tam asked.

*Seems to be in one piece. Can't tell for sure. That blasted chip of yours is a piece of utter crap.*

*Sorry.*

*You should be.*

The inner banter was familiar, comfortable. It was how they always prepared for a fight. It loosened muscles, tightened their connection, began the adrenaline pump from their CPUs.

The warehouse squatted in the shadows of the setting suns, corroded siding, crooked doors and shattered windows giving it an air of decay and neglect.

They hit the double loading bay doors in unison, shoulders slamming the metal aside as if it were paper. Tam let his systems do the scouting, focussing on the first warm body in his sights. He hit the stocky man with the same force he'd used on the doors. The man went flying and crashed into a stack of crates. He crumpled into a heap and didn't get up.

A grunt from his side reassured Tam that he wasn't fighting alone. It was a good feeling. Actually, a fantastic feeling. He turned his attention to the next threat. A big guy, even taller than Tam himself, was abandoning his position in front of a padlocked door. *Hell, yes.* That was the one he wanted.

Tam started for the idiot, a grin of pure anticipation slipping over his face. Damn, but he loved this.

A loud, warning beep slammed into his head. Tam looked up.

*Hellfire and brimstone.*

A pair of bare feet came flying out of the wall. They slammed into the big guy, tangling around the thick neck, and the two figures crashed to the ground. Tam winced when he heard the distinct sound of bone snapping.

The pair had landed at Tam's feet, the body of the airborne assailant completely buried underneath the still, beefy form of the guard. A very familiar squeak made its way out from under the pile.

"What have I told you about patience?" Tam asked.

Another squeak sounded. "Tam? Help!" Fabric rustled as his little lover tried to squirm free from the weight trapping him on the concrete floor. "Tam! Seriously, I can't breathe down here!"

"Maybe you should have thought about that before you launched yourself out of a twelve foot high vent," Tam replied. He bent over and rolled the big body aside, grunting a bit with the effort. Hell, it was one of *those* Teks. All muscle enhancements and steroids. It screwed with their mass, made them weigh about three times more than they should. Terran was lucky he hadn't been squished into a human pancake.

The guard finally dropped to one side, giving Terran enough room to scoot free.

"Dang," his little man panted. "If I had known he was going to fall on me, I might have re-thought the whole jumping from the vent thing."

Terran brushed himself off, yanking his shirt into place, which had inexplicably been wrapped around under his arms, leaving his pale belly exposed. His pretty, blue eyes kept staring at his bare feet.

"You okay, Little Bit?" Tam asked gently.

Suspiciously moist eyes turned up to look at him. "You left me," he accused.

"I know, Bit. And it's a mistake we won't make again."

"Promise?"

"Promise."

Tam's arms were suddenly full of a warm body. He tugged the lithe form close, burying his nose in Terran's hair and just savouring the fragrant, albeit sweaty and a bit dusty, scent of his Terran. A pair of strong arms wrapped around them both, Dai having finished with the clean-up and joining their hug.

"Missed you, baby," Dai whispered.

"Me, too. Both of you. So much."

Terran suddenly pulled back, eyes wide. "Oh! Oh, I have to tell you something." He was practically bouncing on the balls of his feet he was so eager to impart his news. "The guy who's after us! You'll never guess. He was here earlier. It's Carter. You know, that jerkoff from your last job."

"Carter? Erasmus Carter?" Tam didn't know why the information surprised him, but it did. It made a lot of sense, though. A whole lot. The man always did carry a grudge too far.

But that simplified things, it really did. Dai's wicked grin said he was thinking along the same lines.

"Well, hell. That's the best news I've heard all day," Dai announced.

Terran looked at them both like they were crazy. "Carter," he enunciated carefully. "Wealthy? Powerful? Complete sociopath?"

"That's the one," Tam agreed cheerfully.

"And this is good news why?"

"Because we know how to deal with his kind." Dai stroked Terran's bright hair away from his face. "One man is easy to get rid of. It's when you have a whole organisation after you that things get complicated."

"And this is one man in particular that we'll take great pleasure in getting rid of," Tam assured him.

"I still think you're both nuts," Terran said with a little pout.

Tam just had to kiss him. When they parted, breathless and hard, Dai took his turn.

Terran clung to them, a hand wrapped around each of their arms. His blue eyes were glazed with lust, cheeks flushed. "Can we go home now?" he asked plaintively.

"You bet, Little Bit." Tam swung Terran up into his arms, not wanting his treasure to cut up his feet on the way back through the ports.

"You always seem to be losing your shoes," Dai chided.

Terran shrugged. "I had to sacrifice something to get out of the tiny room they shoved me in."

Dai hesitated. "We shouldn't waste any more time here."

"That's okay," Terran said. "I can get new ones. I kind of like where I am."

*Yeah.* Tam agreed with that one hundred percent. Terran in his arms, Daior at his side, they exited the warehouse, blinking in the sudden blaze of light.

# Chapter Twenty-Three

"You always have to go and mess up my perfect plans." Carter scowled ferociously at them, arms folded across his pristine, white suit coat, effectively blocking their path.

He looked, Terran thought with disgust, absurdly annoyed. And what the hell did that bastard have to be annoyed about, anyway? They were the ones who had been kidnapped, chased, harassed and inconvenienced. They were the ones who should be annoyed. Heck, thinking about their ship? Not to mention his jaunt through the crawlspace? Terran was far past annoyed and well into incredibly pissed.

"We live to please," Dai replied dryly.

Tam set Terran on his feet with a sigh.

Terran looked up at him. "Can you please take care of this so we can go home and have wild and wicked sex?"

"That's the plan."

Of course, Terran wasn't the least bit surprised to see that Carter didn't handle his own dirty work. He'd brought along more in his endless supply of mercenaries. No way were they getting past this miniature army of his. The men were fanning out, backing up their leader, although a couple of them didn't seem too happy about it. Well, working for a psycho had its own dangers. He didn't feel sorry for them.

"Where the hell do you get them all?" Dai asked, completely serious. "Damn, I didn't know there was that much muscle for hire in the entire universe, let alone this corner of it. What do you do, go to Mercs-R-Us?"

"Actually," Tam put in, "I think he hired every Malkaian in the universe."

Carter ignored the exchange. "You'll hand over the little splice now."

"No, we won't."

Terran poked Tam in the side.

"Not now, Bit."

Terran poked him again.

"Terran!"

Tam continued trying to stare down Carter. It wasn't working well. The man didn't blink very often. The superior expression on his face made Terran want to cross his eyes and stick out his tongue, just to tweak him.

Since Tam wasn't listening, Terran went for his other man. Tapping was apparently not effective enough, so he slammed his elbow into Dai's gut.

"Ouch! What, Terran?" Daior turned his scowl on the smaller man, rubbing his ribs.

"You've got a communications unit in all that technology of yours, don't you?"

"Sure."

"Well, call the police, then."

Daior raised one eyebrow.

Terran growled in frustration, waving at Carter and his crew. "That much weaponry has *got* to be illegal."

"It's an interstellar port. Everyone's carrying."

"Military grade? And what about kidnapping? Is that legal here?"

Daior sighed but pulled out a small, black box from one of his many pockets anyway.

Carter was clearly through being ignored, though. He snapped an order and his men moved in.

Daior tossed the device to Terran, shoved his bigger bulk in front of the little man and drew his weapons in one smooth motion. Tam, beside him, now had two highly lethal—and illegal—guns in his hands, holding the mercs at bay. Temporarily. At Carter's repeated order, his men swarmed towards them. Tam body-slammed a skinny guy in purple—purple?—armour, Daior kicked another guy in the nuts. Both were firing their weapons almost non-stop. Terran ducked low and began punching the all-purpose emergency code into the Comm unit.

*Stupid, Terran. So stupid. Never take your eyes off the sociopath.*

With Dai and Tam otherwise occupied, Carter had lunged forward, finally deciding to get his own hands dirty. He wrapped his forearm around Terran's neck and pressed a small but lethal-feeling little pistol to Terran's temple. The cold metal seemed to bore a hole through his skull, and Terran shivered. He tugged at Carter, but the man was a heck of a lot stronger than he looked. Terran should have known. Anyone with that much money would have had *some* enhancements put in.

Carter backed up in the direction of the warehouse, clutching Terran in front of him like a shield and seemingly oblivious to the mounting chaos around him. Terran dug his heels into the pavement, trying to slow their progress. Of course, he'd forgotten about his missing boots. He let out another yelp as the rocks ripped into his skin and decided it would be less painful to go back to yanking on the starchy, rough fabric of Carter's suit.

"Enough!" Carter yelled. "It's over."

The mercs stopped almost at once. Dai spun around and started for Carter and Terran.

"I'm taking the splice," Carter stated calmly. "Try to stop me and he'll be missing some body parts. I don't need all of him. An arm or leg here or there won't make any difference."

*It matters to me*, Terran thought indignantly.

Side-by-side with Tam again, Daior's muscles tensed, and he let out a low growl.

Terran furrowed his brow, mind plotting and discarding at rapid speed. Something must have given him away, though—he was told he got this particular little glint in his eyes when he was about to do something stupid. Either way, Tam started to move forward.

"Terran, don't!"

His shout was too late. Terran laid his sharp teeth into the skin of Carter's forearm. Carter shouted, grip loosening. Terran squirmed and went for the kill, knee coming up. Tam and Dai were already moving, Tam for Terran and Daior for Carter's weapon.

They didn't make it. The pop of the gun was almost inaudible over the accompanying shouts and the sounds of running. Tam and Daior both collided with the still-struggling pair, and all four of them hit the ground in a heap.

Sirens ripped through the air and Terran struggled to see what was happening. A number of Carter's men were suddenly slipping away into the shadows.

Those would probably be the licensed mercenaries, the ones who were registered with the Feds. The legitimate ones who didn't really want to risk losing said licenses. The ones remaining were probably underground, modified on the black market and taking whatever jobs they could scrounge up. It was a tough life. If found, they would go to jail regardless, so what difference did a couple of more felonies tacked on make?

Several vehicles pulled up to the warehouse, sirens still blaring with deafening wails, lights flashing brightly on the dingy buildings.

"Everyone, put your weapons down."

The order split the air, calm and commanding. Clearly not local, the officer jumping out of the nearest boxy transport practically screamed Fed. What the heck an officer of the Naturide Federation was doing on this hellhole, Terran didn't know, but he was extremely glad the man was on their side. Feds were hard-nosed bastards and didn't take too kindly to someone breaking laws in front of them. Already his men spread out, gathering the remaining mercs.

"*Dray* Praetis?" the officer called. He sounded worried.

Some random authority figure was yelling in Terran's ear, Dai's legs were practically wrapped around his neck and Terran really, really didn't want to be this close to Carter anymore. He struggled to free himself from the tangle.

"Terran! You all right? Where are you hurt?" Tam, still in the pile of bodies, yanked Terran towards him and started running his hands over the little man's chest, searching frantically for any sign of blood.

"I'm fine!" Terran screeched, trying to wriggle away. "Tam, stop, that tickles!"

The Fed officer skidded to a halt and bent over, panting, hands on his knees. "Oh, thank the Gods," he breathed.

"Do I know you?" Terran asked, peeking over the shoulder of Daior, who was currently trying to squeeze the breath out of him. Tam couldn't stop touching. Terran was feeling a bit queasy, himself. Carter could have…

*Wait. Carter.*

The Fed held out a hand and Tam took it, letting the man pull him to his feet. Dai stood up with Terran still wrapped in his arms.

Carter didn't move, aside from a roll of the head and a loud groan. So, the jerk was still alive. *Pity.*

Terran was pleased to note the idiot had, however, managed to shoot himself in the leg. Go him.

"I'm bleeding," Carter wailed.

"No shit," the Fed said. He looked down at Carter with a distinct lack of sympathy. The man's right pant leg was turning a lovely shade of red, ruining the perfect suit.

In fact, nothing about Carter looked remotely perfect anymore. Aside from the ruination of his clothes, his hair was a mess and dirt streaked across his face. Terran grinned, extremely pleased to note the drops of blood on his arm from where Terran had bitten him. Sharp, pointy teeth did come in handy sometimes.

A couple of additional officers jogged up, guns at their sides, eyes still warily watching the few mercenaries whose escape had been cut off.

"Cuff him," the Fed ordered. "They can patch him up in lockup. If he bleeds to death in the meantime, that's just such a shame."

The officers yanked Carter to his feet and Terran watched them haul off the complaining man.

"Well, that was anticlimactic," Terran commented. His words received disbelieving looks from the three men. He pouted. "Well, it was. No one died."

"Bloodthirsty little thing, isn't he?" the Fed remarked.

"Yep," Daior replied proudly.

"I don't know you," Terran stated. He was still trying to puzzle out not only why a Fed was there, but why and how the Fed had become involved.

"No, but I'm pleased to finally meet you," the officer said, sticking out a hand. Terran shook it, bemused and still wrapped tightly against Daior's side. "First Lieutenant Mark Rosenthal, Naturide Federation Ground Force. I've heard quite a bit about you recently."

"Let me guess," Terran replied, the light finally dawning. And dang but he must be getting tired if it took him that long. "Richard called you in?"

"Indeed, *Dray* Praetis. He informed us of your disappearance and has kept us apprised of the situation ever since. We've had two full units out searching. Fortunately, I was already on-planet attending to another matter when we received word from him that you were here."

"Jerkoff," Dai muttered. "He must still be tracking us."

"I'm glad he was," Tam countered. "For once the ass came in handy."

Rosenthal snorted, the sound rife with amusement, but when Terran looked, the man's face was studiously blank.

"Yeah," Terran agreed. "My brother tends to have that effect on people."

"You don't seem to have needed us, though, except for the clean-up," Rosenthal said.

Daior squeezed Terran warningly. "Baby, what's this *Dray* stuff? And you want to explain why the Feds would care if you went missing?"

"Oh. That." Terran bit his lip. "Well…"

"We're always interested in the kidnapping of royalty," Rosenthal said, eyes reflecting confusion. "Particularly if it happens away from their home planet."

"Royalty?"

Daior sounded distinctly like he was choking on something.

Terran did his best to hide his wince.

"Not exactly," he hedged. "More like…nobility, I guess. Da doesn't rule the planet. Anymore."

"Anymore?" Dai bellowed.

This time Terran heard the aborted laugh, he knew he did. Rosenthal didn't quite manage to hide his amusement as well this time.

"I'll let you three settle things on your own. I have a prisoner to process. Carter's money and connections aren't going to save him this time. Not from a kidnapping charge like this one."

"You're not going to take me back to Richard?" Not that Terran was complaining, heck no. He was just too shocked to keep the words in.

"Your brother ordered me to," Rosenthal admitted. Then his eyes glittered with humour again.

Terran relaxed.

"But your father countered the order," Rosenthal went on. "I'd far rather anger Richard Praetis than Evan Praetis."

Terran would, too. Richard would bluster and bellow a lot. Evan got really cold and…yeah. He got shivers just thinking about it.

Rosenthal's face sobered as he turned to look first Tam, then Daior, in the eyes. "Take good care of him," he said.

Terran scowled. "That sounds more like a threat than advice."

Rosenthal smiled enigmatically, touched his forehead in a brief salute and turned with military precision, already barking orders.

"I like him," Tam stated.

"Can we go home now?"

Exhaustion hit Terran hard and fast. He suddenly wanted nothing more than to curl up with his men and sleep for a couple of days. He didn't care what happened to Carter, or his men, or what his brother was doing, or calling his father or any of the million and one things Terran should probably do. He just wanted to cuddle into a soft bed and let his men hold him.

It had been a really, really long couple of days.

"Absolutely," Tam said. He wrapped his arm around Terran's waist from one side, and Daior did the same from the other.

Tucked between two solid walls of masculinity, Terran let himself relax at long last.

He didn't even care about his bare feet anymore. With his two men supporting most of his weight, he barely even touched the ground. Terran snuggled and let his lovers take care of him.

They were quite good at it, after all.

# Chapter Twenty-Four

Daior was content. Silly, perhaps, but it wasn't a feeling he could remember having very often. He was propped against a mound of pillows on a soft mattress, Terran was in his lap and Tam was on his way back with food. *Yeah, content.* It was nice.

Tam entered the room, padding across the rugs on bare feet, already stripped to the waist. Daior was briefly distracted, admiring the scenery.

"Here, Bit." Tam handed over the small container.

The look of bliss on Terran's face when he opened it up was almost comical.

"Don't I get cheesecake?" Daior grumbled.

"Were you kidnapped and almost shot?" Tam retorted. "I don't think so. No cheesecake for you."

Daior scowled and opened his mouth.

Terran stopped the brewing argument with the simple action of shoving a forkful of dessert at Dai. Daior chewed blissfully. *Ah, cheesecake.* One of life's greatest pleasures.

He squirmed a bit, mind leaping to another of life's greatest pleasures. Terran's firm arse planted against his groin had him revved and ready. As he watched, Tam leaned over and licked stray flecks of creamy dessert off Terran's lips.

"Umm, sweet," Tam hummed.

"Yep, I am," Terran said. He gave a little bounce.

Daior grabbed the thin hips to still him.

"Watch it, baby, I've got plans for that." He thrust his hard cock against Terran's arse to demonstrate.

Honest to Gods, Terran whimpered. Dai loved that sound.

Terran shoved aside the cheesecake in favour of more vigorous activity. He whirled around and gave Dai a sloppy kiss. Like Tam, Dai couldn't resist tasting and licking. And not just his lover, either.

Tam pressed close. "Need you," he said. "Both of you."

"You've got us," Daior promised. He captured Tam's lips while Terran went wandering. Dai nipped at the swollen, pink flesh, the kiss rough and harsh. Sex with both of his lovers was fabulous, but with Tam, Dai could let loose. He worried sometimes about breaking Terran. The man was tough, but small. Tam, on the other hand, could and had taken anything Dai could dish out. And more.

Small hands pressed against both their cheeks, holding them together, Terran licking his way sideways into the kiss.

Dai turned with sudden ferocity, pinning Terran to the bed. "Could have lost you," he said hoarsely.

"I'm not going anywhere," Terran assured him.

"We aren't losing you again," Tam said fiercely. "Not to your brother, not to anyone."

Terran sat back up, face scrunching with a touch of anger. "I wasn't the one who got lost," he pointed out. "You sent me away!"

"Not happening again." Daior pulled Terran close, pressing their lower bodies together. He was shamelessly trying to distract the man, he admitted it. But he felt guilty, thinking about the whole mess. And guilt really wasn't something he was used to.

Judging by the glazed look dropping over Terran's face, his distraction technique was working. Tam growled, flexing his big hands around Dai's waist. *Well, what do you know?* Apparently, Tam could be distracted, too.

It was fast and messy, and in the end, no one even made it inside anyone else. They just rubbed and humped and thrust, grunts and moans filling the air, lust coming fast and furious. It wasn't as much about getting off as it was touching, tasting, reassuring all three of them they were safe and together.

Daior's release was sudden, not explosive but drawn out and consuming. His cum mixed with his lovers', coating their bodies and blending their scents. They dropped together in a heap, Dai not sure where one of them ended and the other began. He loved it.

The words popped out before he even knew they were coming.

"I love you."

He nearly bit off his own tongue. Damn it, that was *not* supposed to come out. He was the big, tough, grumpy one. He didn't do touchy, feely—

"I love you, too," Terran whispered, squeezing Dai tightly. "Both of you."

Daior looked over at Tam. The big man didn't say anything, but his mouth tilted up at the corners and his eyes shone a bit suspiciously. Daior swallowed, feeling the love in Tam's touch, in the soft kiss he placed on first Dai, then Terran.

Daior yanked the covers out from underneath Terran and wrapped them all up together, not caring that they were messy and sticky. He was tired and ready to just snuggle for a while. Terran's snuggling fetish had started to rub off on him. Not, of course, that he was going to be admitting it anytime soon. Just like he wasn't going to be saying those three blasted words out loud very often. And certainly never outside of this particular room.

Dai was just starting to drop off for a nice little nap when Terran shot up, yanking the covers away. "Da! I need to contact him. He's probably frantic."

Tam, who had given a startled jump at Terran's shout, dropped his head back onto the pillow and closed his eyes. Dai grumbled and tugged his corner of the blanket back over his head. Damn, how could their baby even move, let alone think?

"Rosenthal will have called," he mumbled. "Plenty of time to tell your dad the whole story later."

"But—"

"Sleep," Dai demanded, snaking his hand out to jerk Terran back down onto the pile of sweaty limbs and entwined torsos. "Worry later."

"But—"

"Terran."

Terran heaved a put-upon sigh but settled back down. He shot back up again a second later. Like a damn jack-in-the-box, Dai thought irritably. Stupid things always creeped him out.

"Richard! He'll be looking for me. He was already tracking us and—"

"Dickwad isn't a problem anymore." This time Dai's words came out in more of a growl, his temper fraying. Next to him, Tam just closed his eyes and let them work it out. *Traitor.* "Now sleep!"

Terran finally gave in, snuggling his warm little body between their much larger ones. "Promise?"

"Promise," Dai said around an annoyed sigh.

"'Kay," came the sleepy reply.

Terran was snoring softly less than thirty seconds later. Dai's lips quirked in amusement. He rolled over a bit so his free hand could stroke along the expanse of naked skin sprawled next to him. He didn't know whose skin it was, didn't really care. He had his two lovers and that was all that really mattered.

Then Dai let his own eyes drift close. He was tired. Exhausted. Utterly and completely drained. Best to catch a few minutes of sleep while he could. He had the feeling he was going to need it.

As he curled around Terran, letting his body sink into the mattress, he couldn't help thinking that it was all worth it, though. The kidnapping, the fighting, the planet-hopping. All of it. Any amount of trouble was worth it as long as he got to join these two men in bed every night.

For once, getting snagged had turned out to be a good thing. He dropped off to sleep, thanking whatever Gods were listening for sending his very own cat flying into his life.

The cat that was currently curled into a ball, purring his little heart out.

# Epilogue

"What are you doing?" Jackson tried to inject the right balance of command in his voice without sounding overly interested in the answer to his question. It was a tricky thing, getting information out of Richard. Hell, lately, talking to the man was like trying to navigate an active asteroid storm. One wrong step and the whole conversation would blow out from under you.

"I'm tailing the *Farion*, what else?" Richard snapped. His long fingers moved nimbly over the keyboard, confidence written in every line of his well-built frame.

Jackson was of the personal opinion that Richard could do with a little less self-confidence.

"I thought we'd discussed this already. We're leaving Terran to his new men. Besides, you're needed back on Altaireon."

"Father just wants to yell at me. Again. Terran is my responsibility and I don't entirely trust those new men of his."

Jackson rubbed his forehead, feeling another headache building. Gods save him. One of these days he was going to retire, he really was. Then Richard would be someone else's problem.

Jackson ran his hand over his bristly hair, picturing the iron grey that had almost completely replaced his once blond buzz cut. Riding herd on the Praetis brothers was hard on a body. He felt nearly a decade older than his current fifty-three.

"Richard."

When Jackson was roundly ignored, his temper started to rise. "*Captain,*" he snapped.

Richard swivelled to bestow an angry glare of his own. "What?"

"Enough. I don't know what the hell has got into you in the last few years, but I've had enough. As has your father. We're returning to Altaireon and leaving Terran to Jannssen and Mathews."

Richard turned his back to Jackson again. "I don't like failing," he muttered.

Jackson had to strain to catch the words, and for a minute he thought his hearing was going, along with his hair.

So that was what this was about. Richard and that damn perfectionist streak. It had been causing problems from the first day they'd left Altaireon years ago.

Jackson dropped into the co-pilot's chair and joined Richard in staring blankly out at space.

"Do you really think he's happy with them?" Again, the words were spoken quietly.

Well, at least Richard still felt comfortable enough to open up. Jackson would bet, though, that he was the only one to ever see this side of Richard. The caring, vulnerable side. And he only saw it because he'd been Richard's mentor, teacher and companion since the boy was thirteen.

"Yes," Jackson replied. "I think he's very happy with them."

Richard's hand hovered over the control panel then pulled away again. "I just…I've been looking after him for so long. I'm not sure I know how to stop."

"He doesn't need looking after anymore, Richard. He hasn't in a long time."

"Terran hates me, doesn't he?"

"No. But he will if you don't back off."

In a jerky move, Richard cancelled his current course. Jackson hid a satisfied smile.

"I want my brother back," Richard said. "We used to be close, you know? I lost that somewhere along the way and I don't know how to fix it."

"Start by remembering you're not his father. Or his keeper. Or any of the dozens of other roles you've tried to take on."

"I worry."

Ah, there it was. The heart of the issue. Aside from his perfectionist streak, Richard's other major flaw—or asset, depending on how he was applying it—was his complete and utter devotion to family. He would do anything to ensure their safety.

Jackson called Richard's name softly until he was sure he had the younger man's complete attention. "He's not a child anymore. You can let go. Whatever Terran can't handle himself, his new men are more than capable of taking care of."

Richard's lips quirked. It wasn't quite a smile, but it was closer to one than Jackson had seen in months.

"I imagine they are."

"Then point us home."

It was far past time for Richard to get a life of his own. And Jackson was going to see that he did just that. Whether Richard agreed or not.

# About the Author

Born and raised in the middle of the Midwest, I have always been a dreamer. More often than not I could be found with my nose buried in a book (many of which I had to sneak past my parents). It wasn't long before I started trying my hand at writing more of the stories I loved. After years of penning tales that rarely left the hard drive of my computer, I discovered M/M romance. As with all genres, it wasn't long before my own characters started to take shape.

There is little I love more than wandering new places and, on occasion, entirely new worlds with my characters. They can range from cowboys to Victorian noblemen, accountants to shapeshifters, and everything in between. I write mainly m/m romance, usually with paranormal or fantasy elements. I willingly follow my characters wherever they decide to go, sometimes with unusual results. I have little control over their actions – any naughty behaviour is all their doing!

K.M. Mahoney loves to hear from readers.

You can find her contact information, website details and author profile page at http://www.total-e-bound.com.

# Total-E-Bound Publishing